J

A CRY
FOR HOME

BEULAH NEVEU

BeNeveu Words Inc.
PUBLISHING COMPANY

BeNeveu Words Inc.

Publishing Company
BeNeveu Words Inc. Publishing Company
Rosenberg, TX 77471

For information
BeNeveu Words Inc. Publishing Company
beneveuwords@yahoo.com

ISBN-13 DIGIT: 978-0-692-33172-9
ISBN-10 DIGIT: 0692331727
Library of Congress Control Number: 2014920288
Manufactured in the United States of America

First Edition

Visit us at beneveuwords4you.com

ALSO AVAILABLE
FROM BEULAH NEVEU

Bracie

Bracie is a Christian love story about faith, family and friends. It tells the story of a quest for true love and the uncertainty of the very thing that is being searched for. It's a story about the strength and unity of family in the good times and the not so good.

Bracie is surrounded by family and friends, yet she is still lonely. Her desire to fill that void leaves her vulnerable to the one thing she has not learned to control-PASSION. Through a computer error she reconnects with someone from the past. He takes her on a secret whirlwind romance, until one night it all blows up in her face. After struggling to put her life back on track Bracie's faith and quiet strength is put to the test when greed and jealousy threatens her happiness.

Tyler is handsome and rich. True love is something he does not think is possible until he meets Bracie. She takes him back to the simple way of life, and that makes him happiest of all.

Tyler and Bracie have to make a decision. Will their relationship be able to weather the storms of Hollywood? Can true love really conquer all when two different life styles are forced to go public and contend with opposition from both sides?

Visit *beneveuwords4you.com* for more information about Bracie and upcoming titles from Beulah Neveu

ACKNOWLEGMENTS

First, I would like to thank God for blessing me with the gift of writing. I am thankful for the opportunity to be His vessel in writing my second novel. I am so grateful that God has given me a new light into Bracie's story while teaching me that the greatest legacy we can leave is the life we live for Him.

I would like to thank my husband Thomas Jr. for being my inspiration and strength. I thank him for his love and support, but mostly I thank him for covering me in prayer as I embark on each new endeavor.

I would like to thank my mother Verna LaCour for being my greatest example of living a godly life. I would like to thank her for teaching me that with God all things really are possible. I would like to thank my children Verna2, DeAnthany Sr., DeJuan Sr. and DeRaymond Sr. for their love, continued support and for always believing in me.

I would like to thank my grandchildren for their support and encouragement. A special thanks to DeAnthany Jr. for being my little manager.

I would like to acknowledge my daughters-in-law Romesha, Tina and Tiffany for loving my sons and encouraging me. I would like to thank Janae Hampton for being a wonderfully patient editor. I would also like to acknowledge a few people who have pushed me into all that God has for me. They are listed in no particular order: The ladies of Woman2Woman, my sisters Myranda Gipson and Lolita Woods and her husband Curtis, my brothers Donald and Albert Hall, Robert Simms, Yolanda Samuels, Doug and Ronda James, Pastors Eric and Phyllis Wiggins, my pastors, Dr. Gusta Booker Sr. and Pastor Ronald Booker Sr., and the Late Dr. Theola Booker.

I would like to thank Cathy Ozan, Verna Hall and Jennifer Lee for their helpful insight while reading and critiquing *A Cry For Home.*

I would like to thank everyone who has supported me, encouraged me, and prayed for me.

Last, but certainly not least, I would like to give special thanks to Carl Eatmon of Darmik Management/Entertainment and Author Keith Thomas Walker for mentoring me on this journey. I thank you for your leadership and guidance. Thank you for the constructive criticism that was done in love, but mostly I thank you for your patience and your prayers. Without you, I know my journey would not be as rewarding as it is.

Be Blessed and Enjoy!

A CRY FOR HOME

FOREWORD

I had the pleasure of meeting Mrs. Beulah Neveu after registering for a conference in Houston last year. She was a new author with only one book under her belt. Noticing I had published quite a few novels, Beulah reached out to me with questions about the writing business. I receive similar inquiries on a regular basis, but never has it led to something as meaningful as the friendship Beulah and I now share.

It's important to note that most authors, especially independent authors who still have a day job, are very busy people. But I have no regrets about the time I've spent corresponding with Beulah. I would have to say that God led this author to me, and He also touched my heart, so that I would not turn my back on her.

Over the last year and a half, I have read Beulah's books, and she has read all of mine. Her fascination with my stories is equal to the fascination I felt the first time I read Bracie. Time and time again, Beulah has surprised me with her passion for writing and her insight. I am grateful and honored to have been a part of the growth of this talented writer.

I hope you enjoy her second novel, *A Cry for Home*, and I pray that God will continue to bless this author. Anyone can have a dream. I'm repeatedly proud of Beulah for pursuing hers and bringing them to fruition.

Keith Thomas Walker

A CRY FOR HOME

Chapter 1

Cherralyn sat behind the large desk. She'd moved into Bracie's office three months ago and was still taken away by the beauty and warmth that was there. She had left the picture of Tyler and Bracie sitting on the bureau right where Bracie kept it. She wanted to always remember the hard work and love that had started the youth center. It had been 11 years since Bracie had walked into her life and changed everything for the better. Bracie was the first example of a true Christian, god fearing, and God loving woman that Cherralyn ever had step in and show her that she too was beautiful. Bracie took the time to talk to Cherralyn about her faith and love for God, as well as her decision to save herself for her husband to be, Tyler Shaw. But it wasn't just Cherralyn that Bracie and Tyler had touched. Their lives and their marriage had served as a ministry to their entire communities, leaving everyone devastated by their loss. It had been six months since Bracie and Tyler's untimely passing and Cherralyn missed her everyday as she stood, as CEO and director of the center, which served as the very place where Bracie had touched her life. She and Vanessa, the assistant director, had both gained insurmountable insight from having been touched by Bracie and had made the decision to change the center's name to The Bracie Shaw Outreach Center soon. The dedication was a month away, and there was a lot of work to do to have everything in order.

Cherralyn got up and walked towards the door just as it flew open. James stood in front of her ready to scream. Before he did, she spoke, "Calm down."

"She's at it again!" he said. James tried all he could to keep his twin sister Jasmine out of trouble.

"Where is she?" Cherralyn asked calmly.

"I don't know. She knew we were having grief counseling today. She said she wasn't coming."

James shook his head. He wanted so much more for his sister, she seemed to be angry at the world, since their parents were killed five months ago in a car accident. Being uprooted from their home and moving to California didn't help her in dealing with her grief.

Cherralyn took James by the shoulder and walked with him to the classroom. She attended the grief class most of the time. Everyone thought it was to encourage the children, but really she needed the spiritual comfort and guidance as well. She was still having a hard time handling Bracie's sudden illness and death. Being in the class gave her strength.

When the class ended, Cherralyn told James to call her when Jasmine came home or called. She returned to her office and said a prayer for Jasmine. Cherralyn thought about the day their aunt brought them into the center. James stood tall, and she could tell there was something good and strong in him. His sister stood next to him with a blank stare.

Cherralyn took a deep breath, because she knew the pain behind that look all too well. James was very polite while Jasmine did all she could to seem hard and tough. They sat in her office and talked about their parents' accident and moving to California.

After their thirty minute visit, Cherralyn knew that Jasmine was angry with God for taking her parents. She was raised in a Christian home, but she had turned away from God after their deaths. Jasmine was a good person, and she was only seventeen years old. Cherralyn knew she had to find a way to help her before it was too late.

●●●●●●●

Jasmine and Shayna were friends. They met at school where they were both seniors and both wanted things to go back to the way they were. The girls were sitting on a park bench laughing at people as they passed by. They had been drinking and were feeling kind of tipsy.

Michael walked up and kissed both girls on the mouth. He paid more attention to Jasmine because he wanted her to feel special. He offered both of them more to drink. Shayna told him they didn't want any more. Michael didn't argue, because he knew he could get with Shayna when he needed to. He sat down and joined in on their antics just as James approached. He walked up to his sister and said, "It's time to go home."

Jasmine gave him a cold look. "I don't have a home here," she retorted.

He stood his ground with her. "If you don't come with me, I promise to make a scene." James knew his sister hated being embarrassed and made the center of attention. She stood up and stumbled with her first couple of steps. James held on to her and helped her to his car.

Once they were home, Jasmine showered and entered the kitchen. Their aunt Janice sat in the den while the twins talked. James looked at his sister.

"Why do you hang out with those two? They don't mean you any good," he said.

"They're my friends," she replied as she took a plate of food from him and sat down to eat.

"With friends like that, you better not have any enemies."

"Don't start," she said and started eating.

"That Michael guy is up to no good. He wants you, Jasmine. You can't see that?"

She glanced up at her brother, touched by his concern. "I know, James. I'm not crazy. I'm still a virgin, and I plan to stay that way."

James and their aunt both gave a quiet sigh of relief.

Jasmine finished her food and washed her plate. She and James sat at the table to do their homework. They enjoyed times like this. James wished it could always be this way. Jasmine was usually well-behaved, but when she missed their parents, instead of talking, she struck out at everyone around her, except James.

Janice walked over and asked if they needed help. They both answered no. She was proud of her nephew and niece. They were very smart and talented. Both could sing and play the piano, but Jasmine had a special gift of art. She seldom painted or drew anymore, because it was the gift favored by their mother. Janice bid the twins goodnight and went to bed.

"Why do you dislike her?" James asked his sister.

"Dislike who?" Jasmine asked, startled by his question.

"Aunt Janice."

"I don't dislike her. I love her. She's our auntie. She reminds me so much of Mama. But sometimes, when I look at her, it reminds me that Mama's gone."

James walked over and gave his sister a hug.

"You should let her know how you feel, Jasmine. She thinks you don't like her."

Jasmine had never thought about that.

"Okay," was all she said.

James touched her on the shoulder as she started to leave the kitchen. Jasmine turned back.

"I love you, sis. Always remember that," he told her and gave her another hug.

●●●●●●●

Shayna sat in the garage of her cousin's home, thinking about how much her life had changed. Her older cousin, Latoya had taken her in when she had no place else to go but it was understood that her main dwelling place would be the garage, turned efficiency room, outside. Sometimes Shayna felt so alone. She had met her friend Jasmine at school, where they grew close as the two new girls in the senior class. Later, when they met at the youth center, they found they had even more in common, they were both grieving the tragic loss of a parent. When she was out with her friends she could feel happy and normal again, but once she returned home, it was back to reality.

Though Latoya was five years older than Shayna, growing up the two had been very close. Their mothers were sisters and best friends, so the two were always together. It was Latoya who taught Shayna how to carry herself as a young lady. She took her to have her first manicure and pedicure and they shared all of their secrets. Shayna had always wanted to be just like her big cousin whom she looked at more like a big sister.

After graduation Latoya had left the small city where they had grown up together to attend a college in California. While there she met Richard and the two were married less than a year after graduation. When Richard's grandfather passed and left him a small fortune, Latoya begin acting differently and hadn't been the same since. When her aunt passed away, after battling a long illness, pressure from her mother had forced her to take in her little cousin. But, Latoya believed that anyone who wasn't wealthy was beneath her, including members of her own family, including Shayna.

Richard, however, was more compassionate than his wife and was more than willing open his home to Shayna, but Latoya had used Shayn's grief to convince him that the young girl, wanted to live in the garage space, to be alone and have her privacy. He didn't want to pry, so though he was disappointed he kept his distance and let Shayna have her space to grieve her loss.

This living arrangement was also kept a secret from Latoya's own mother. If she knew the way Shayna was being treated she would have been livid.

And Shayna, just took it all in stride, biding her time, till graduation when she could get away from Latoya and never look back. She reflected on all this and more as she prepared to meet Michael for a late night rendezvous. She knew he wasn't the type of boy she should be messing around with, but there were very few people in her life that seemed to believe she was worth anything at all, and Michael was one of them. She wasn't crazy about his new found attraction for Jasmine, but for now he was all she had.

Chapter 2

James missed his parents, but he was also grateful to his Aunt Janice for taking them in. Their aunt had doted on them since they were babies. James, Jasmine and their parents would all come to California on their family trips.

He remembered their first trip to Disney Land at the age of five. He and Jasmine talked about that summer vacation for years. Even as teenagers, they loved coming to visit their aunt. They even loved her church. The pastor and members were friendly and made them feel at home when they moved here. Some of them had watched James and Jasmine grow up between visits. They all knew Janice loved her sister, and she was crazy about the twins.

James was happy to be with his aunt. Right now, his only wish was for his sister to get herself together.

●●●●●●●

Jasmine and Shayna were riding around in Shayna's car. Her cousin never let her forget how much she had to pay to have her mother's car shipped here from Texas for her. Latoya was upset when Richard paid the car off and added Shayna to their insurance. He felt Shayna should not have to worry with car notes and insurance. She was 17, and her focus should be on school and her friends.

The girls stopped to hang out and get a bite to eat with some of their other friends. Most of the teenagers met at Fast But Fit Burgers. The diner was average in size. It had nine small booths and extra space to sit at the take out counter. The front wall of the diner was two extra large windows. It was always neat, and because of the friendly staff and atmosphere it was always crowded. The service was usually slow, but the food was delicious. They ordered sodas and shared a large order of fries. They were having a good time until they saw Michael drive up.

"I can't stand him," Natalia said.

The other girls looked up and saw Michael as he passed by the window.

"He's so cute," one of them said.

"He knows it, too!" another replied.

"He's also no good," Natalia said in disgust. "He got my sister pregnant and then said it wasn't his."

All of the other girls were surprised by that news, especially Shayna.

"But your sister is younger than we are," Jasmine said.

Shayna sat quietly, upset to learn that she was not the only girl he was sleeping with. Michael sat at the table across from them. He wore starched navy blue dockers and a white buttoned down polo shirt. He had on navy loafers with no socks. He was six feet tall and had a body that would make most college athletes envious. He leaned back against the booth he occupied alone and winked at Natalia. She turned her head and continued talking.

"My sister had a miscarriage and she's been withdrawn ever since."

"They have a grief class at the youth center once a week," Jasmine said. "Maybe it would help her if she goes."

"Thank,, I'll tell my mom," Natalia replied.

Jasmine didn't know why she volunteered the information but was glad she did.

"Ask for Ms. Cherralyn," she said and changed the subject as the waiter brought their food to the table.

"I want to holler at my brother," Jasmine said as James walked in and passed their table. She got her drink and went to sit with him. They were talking when one of the waiters walked to their table with books in his arms.

"Stephen, this is my sister Jasmine," James said, introducing them. "Jasmine, this is Stephen. I am tutoring him for the geometry and biology exams."

Stephen stuck out his hand to shake Jasmine's. When she returned the gesture, he gave her the brightest smile she had ever seen.

"It's nice to meet you, Jasmine. It's good to finally know my favorite customer's name," he said with the smile still on his face.

She blushed and removed her hand from his. Jasmine stood up, looked at Stephen, and smiled.

"I'll see you at the house," she said to James.

"Okay, I'll be home in about an hour," he replied.

Jasmine walked back to the table where all of the girls were watching her.

"Those are the two most handsome guys in school," Shayna said giggling. All of the other girls agreed.

Michael watched the exchange between Jasmine and Stephen, and he didn't like it. He ignored everyone at the table except Jasmine as he passed. He nodded at her and kept walking to his car.

Michael did not attend school where the girls were enrolled. He'd gotten kicked out of high school and left his dad's home his senior year because of disciplinary problems. That was two years ago. Michael couldn't claim a permanent address as his own. He lived with which ever friend allowed him to stay, for as long as they allowed him to stay. No matter how rough things got Michael knew if all else failed he could depend on his friend Terrance to give him a place to lay his head and make him feel at home, for a while. He got into his car and went to hang out with some of his friends.

Michael didn't know why he called them *friends* when they were always too busy to really care. They didn't know his escapade with a minor had almost landed him in jail. They all thought he had one girl he was trying to impress. No one knew but him and Terrance.

"Toss me a beer," he said to Terrance, later that night when he had returned home. Michael popped the tab and drank half the can in one pull.

"What's up with you?" Terrance asked him.

Michael didn't answer.

"You still don't want to talk? I hope you're staying out of trouble," Terrance told him as he walked into the bathroom to do a last check in the mirror. He looked at his reflection and smiled. He stood 5 feet and 11 and a half inches counting in his half inch afro. He kept it neatly cut with a razor sharp edge up. His skin was smooth all over except the thin mustache above his lip. Terrance made sure his salmon colored buttoned down shirt was wrinkle free. He chose the salmon shirt because it made his caramel skin look even creamier. He checked out his dark grey slacks and ran his hand down the starched crease. He smiled again and walked back into the room and stood in front of Michael, who still did not answer as he sank down in the chair and thought about Shayna and Jasmine. Shayna was a virgin when he first slept with her. He knew she was but still felt it was not in him to be the gentle man that she really needed. He used her vulnerability to get what he wanted. He saw that same vulnerability in Jasmine's eyes.

He decided he would be more caring with her. She was beautiful, and there was something about her that he had not quite figured out yet. He thought about Shayna. She could be beautiful too, but there was bitterness in her pain.

Terrance continued to look at Michael deep in thought. When he realized he wasn't going to answer him, he turned towards the door. "Be careful my friend. Be careful," Terrance said and left.

Chapter 3

Vanessa and Cherralyn had only a few days to make sure everything was in order for the center's dedication ceremony. They were going over some paperwork when her assistant, Melanie entered the conference room.

"Cherralyn, a family is here to see you," she said.

Cherralyn looked up from her paperwork. "Do they have an appointment?" She thought a minute. "I know I cleared my calendar."

"No, ma'am, they don't have an appointment. The mother said Jasmine sent them."

Cherralyn got up and went to greet the family. "Hello, my name is Cherralyn Gray. I'm the director here at the center. How may I help you?" she asked the mother as she reached out to shake her hand.

"My name is Maria, and these are my daughters Natalia and Juliana," she said.

"Come, we can talk in my office," Cherralyn said as she led the way there. She opened the door and asked them to have a seat. Cherralyn noticed the

mother relaxed as she began to talk. Maria explained
how Juliana had become depressed after getting
pregnant at 16 years old and then having a miscarriage.

When their visit was over, Cherralyn told Juliana
she would see her in the grief class the following week.
She invited them to the center's dedication ceremony
Saturday morning, and they promised to be there.

The days seem to fly by as everyone worked to get
the center ready. By noon on Saturday, the front lawn
of the center was filled with press and over 200 people.
Vanessa walked up to the podium to start the ceremony.
After her introduction Bracie's pastor, from Houston
offered the opening prayer.

Vanessa talked about Bracie's first time at the
center.

"One of the young ladies from that first class was
mentored by Mrs. Shaw and is now the C.E.O. and
director of the center. Please put your hands together
for Cherralyn Gray."

While everyone clapped, Vanessa stepped aside
and Cherralyn walked up to the microphone. She told
how Bracie's warmth and love for God saved her. She
became emotional as she reflected on Bracie's strength
and humility. As Cherralyn finished, she told everyone
that Bracie Shaw was her example of a faithful woman
of God. She thanked her family for allowing Bracie to
share her life, her love, and her legacy with them in
California. Her family felt proud of the love and
kindness the people of California displayed for her.

Bracie's mother and children were each given a few minutes to speak.

The mayor of the city, along with Cherralyn and Vanessa, cut the ribbon to the front door of the newly named center. Once everyone was standing inside, Cherralyn got all of their attention.

"Before we tour the center, I would like for Bracie's children to come forward, please."

Vanessa and everyone looked puzzled because this was not on the program.

Cherralyn spoke through her tears. "Today we are not only honoring Bracie Shaw, but her husband Tyler. She always let us know that he was her support, strength and encourager. For all that knew them, they got a chance to see God's example of love in marriage lived out through them. Today they are in heaven smiling down on us. As we dedicate this center, we pay homage to both Tyler and Bracie Shaw. A picture of them will always hang here in the Welcoming Area to remind us of God's gift to us through them."

Cherralyn asked Bracie's daughter Kirnette to step forward to help unveil the portrait. It was beautiful. There wasn't a dry eye in the center as Bracie's sons Anthany, Joe'Al and Raymond mounted the painting on the wall.

Janice smiled as she and the twins stood together holding hands as the portrait was hung. She knew Bracie well and was very thankful for her starting the center, because now it was helping her family to heal.

Jasmine saw Natalia and her family and went to say hello.

Bracie's children were standing in front of the portrait when one of the guests walked up. "She was very beautiful," he said.

They all turned at once and said, "Thank you."

He smiled at Kirnette. "My God, you look just like her," he said.

She smiled back. "Yes, I do huh? I just pray my family thinks as loving of me as we do her," Kirnette answered him.

All of Tyler and Bracie's close friends were there, and they were very happy to see her family and friends from Houston. The last time they were all together was Tyler's funeral. Carl and Shanelle two of his closest friends, had him laid to rest in a private cemetery next to Bracie in Houston.

They all toured the center together and ended up back in the Welcoming Center in front of the portrait. Cherralyn approached the group.

"We will continue to run the center in her honor," she said. "Her life was her sermon on love, compassion and hope." She hugged each one of Bracie's children and went back to bid farewell to the rest of the visitors.

It was well into the evening when the last of the guests left. The youth stayed to help clean up and put everything back in place. They talked about the dedication the entire time they cleaned. Those who knew the Shaws told their stories of love, healing and the hope they gave.

Once everyone left, Vanessa told Cherralyn to go on home. She said she would stay and lock up. Shanelle walked over to Vanessa. They laughed and talked as they walked to the front of the center.

"The ceremony was wonderful. You and Cherralyn did an excellent job," Shanelle said.

"Thank you," Vanessa replied as she walked to the portrait. For the first time since their deaths, she cried. Shanelle hugged and comforted her. She understood Vanessa's pain because she missed their friends too.

Chapter 4

Jasmine knew she should be home by now, it was close to midnight. But Shayna didn't have a curfew, and she wasn't ready to leave the party. Jasmine stepped outside and called James.

"Where are you?" he asked, "and why do you keep doing crazy things like this?"

Jasmine expected him to be upset. "We're at a party, and Shayna's not ready to leave," she answered.

James was angry at his sister. "Jasmine, you should have known better. It's a school night. Try again and call me back."

Jasmine felt bad. "Okay," she said and hung up. She walked away from the house and started down the street.

Stephen drove by and slowed down. He backed up. "Jasmine?"

She looked into the car. "Stephen, what's up?"

"What are you doing out so late?" he asked.

"Waiting for my ride, but she's not ready to leave yet."

"I'd be glad to take you home," he said.

Jasmine got in the car and left a message on Shayna's phone.

"Your brother is probably worried about you."

"No, angry is more like it." She took a deep breath and let it out slowly. "How did you do on your exams?" she asked, genuinely concerned.

"Very well, thanks to your brother," he answered.

They talked the entire ride. When they pulled up in front of the house, Jasmine called James and told him she was outside. He opened the door and waved at Stephen.

"We were worried about you!" he said as soon as she stepped inside.

"I'm sorry, but it wasn't my fault this time," Jasmine said. "I told Shayna I was ready to go around ten. I had already started walking when Stephen drove by."

Janice walked out of her room and stood between the twins. "Jasmine, I understand this time it wasn't your fault, but you have to do better than this. I haven't said anything because I know you're missing your parents. You need to get help, so I'm telling you not to miss anymore grief classes with your brother. Have I made myself clear?" she asked sternly.

Jasmine looked at her aunt and answered, "Yes, ma'am."

"Now take a shower and go to bed. You two have school tomorrow." Janice turned and left them both standing in the hallway. James wanted to grab their aunt and hug her for finally putting her foot down.

•••••••

For the next several weeks, Jasmine was on her best behavior. One afternoon Shayna came over to her house to visit.

"What happened to you?" Jasmine asked as she looked at the bruises on her face.

"Some girls jumped me," she said softly with her head down.

"For what?" Jasmine asked.

"They said to stay away from Michael and to leave him alone," Shayna told her.

Jasmine was livid! "Where did they jump you?" she asked angrily.

"At the store," Shayna said.

Jasmine grabbed her by the arm. "Let's go! I need you to show me who did this."

James stood there listening. "It's not your battle Jasmine. Stay out of it."

She rolled her eyes at him on her way out of the door with Shayna in tow. Minutes later they pulled into a spot at the store where the girls had jumped Shayna a few days earlier. It didn't take long for the girls to make an appearance. Jasmine wasn't afraid of the rough looking girls, but could see why Shayna felt intimidated by them. Both girls were very muscular and had tattoos on their arms. They wore large braids in their hair and one had on jeans that sagged off of her behind.

"There they are." Shayna pointed at two girls as they crossed the parking lot. They got out of the car and Jasmine made sure her shoes were tied as she adjusted her clothes. She approached the girls.

"Excuse me."

The girls turned. "What do you want?"

"I want you to keep your hands off of my friend," Jasmine said.

"What friend?!"

By that time, Shayna walked up.

"So you went and got pretty girl for backup?" they said, making fun of both Shayna and Jasmine. "We said stay away from Mike, and that's what we meant!" they said angrily as they walked up to Shayna.

"No, *you* tell Michael to stay away from us!" Jasmine told them with the same attitude.

One girl reached to hit Shayna, and Jasmine knocked her hand down.

"Move back Shayna, I got this."

The two girls charged Jasmine. She slapped one and kicked the other. Before Shayna could react, Jasmine had beaten both girls up and had them on the ground. They never got a chance to touch her.

"Let's get out of here," Jasmine said.

Shayna got in the car and drove Jasmine home.

"I will always have your back," Jasmine told her.

Shayna kept looking at Jasmine, wondering what other secrets her friend had hidden.

●●●●●●●

Little by little, Jasmine and Shayna settled down from their mischief. They both attended grief counseling at the center. Shayna started going to church every Sunday, but Jasmine still would not go.

One Sunday after his sermon, Pastor Jones asked James to sing *Precious Lord*. Because it was one of his mother's favorite songs, Janice asked if he was sure he could handle it. James nodded yes. He went to the podium and sang until his heart was full. James stretched his hand toward heaven and sang as tears flowed down his face.

Shayna's heart was full, for it was also her mother's favorite song. She surrendered her life to Christ that Sunday when James finished singing. Stephen sat and lifted his hands to God in praise and thanksgiving. Janice watched the children honor and worship God and wished Jasmine would come back to church.

In the next few weeks, Shayna started spending more of her time with James and Stephen. Jasmine was trying to figure out if Shayna liked Stephen or her brother. She liked Stephen too, and she didn't want to interfere if he and Shayna were a couple.

As their senior year came to an end, prom and graduation was all everyone talked about. One day Jasmine and Shayna were at Fast But Fit Burgers talking about prom dresses.

"We need dates," Shayna said laughing.

"Who are you going with, James or Stephen?" Jasmine asked curiously.

Shayna stopped laughing and looked at her friend. "I thought *you* liked Stephen. I would love to go with your brother, but he wouldn't want to go with someone like me."

Jasmine knew Shayna was serious by the tone in her voice. "What do you mean someone like you?"

Before Shayna could answer, Michael walked up and kissed her on the mouth. When he tried to kiss Jasmine, she turned her head. Michael turned his attention to Shayna.

"What's up?" he asked, trying to seem innocent.

"Your girls jumped Shayna," Jasmine said getting upset.

"Yeah, and I heard you took care of it," he retorted, dropping the innocent act.

Jasmine glared at him. "Somebody had to!"

Michael looked at Jasmine angrily. He stepped towards her, thinking she would flinch.

"I wish you would!" Jasmine said, still upset and not backing down.

Michael returned his attention to Shayna. "I'm sorry about that. It won't happen again," he said smiling.

Shayna didn't react to his words like he wanted her to, and that upset him. "Remember who cares about you and who's been there for you Shayna!" He looked down at her with a frown and walked away.

"That is a fool if ever I saw one," Jasmine said. "Stay away from him Shayna."

When Jasmine started talking about the prom again, Shayna seemed disinterested. Stephen watched as he stood behind the counter. When the girls got up to leave, he called Jasmine to the counter. He seemed very nervous.

"What's up Stephen?" she asked.

"Would you like to go to the prom with me?" His face lit up when Jasmine answered him.

"Yes, I would."

"Great! We'll talk colors later," he said still smiling.

"Okay, I have to go now. Shayna's waiting for me."

Stephen nodded and went back to work.

Shayna knew before Jasmine could say anything that Stephen had asked her to the prom. Both girls were unusually quiet on the way to Jasmine's house. When they got there, Jasmine asked her what was wrong. The real problem was Shayna wanted to go to the prom with James, but she knew he wouldn't ask her, since she had been messing around with Michael. She didn't want to tell Jasmine any of her thoughts about James. Instead she responded, "I'm ok, just thinking about the prom," which was partly true.

Chapter 5

Prom night finally arrived and they were all very excited. Jasmine and Stephen chose royal blue and silver for their colors. She wore a long royal blue strapless formal gown with silver accessories and silver sandals. She had her hair pulled back with small curls hanging down on each side of her face. She was naturally beautiful so her only make up was lip gloss and a light coat of eye shadow. Stephen wore a grey tuxedo with a white shirt and royal blue bow tie. He had a royal blue and white handkerchief folded neatly in his pocket. His hair was cut into a short afro with an edge up so clean and neat most young men would die for it.

James chose emerald green and brown for his prom attire. He sported a dark brown tuxedo, with an ivory shirt and emerald green bow tie. He opted for an ivory rose in his pocket instead of a handkerchief. His hair was cut very close to his head so the waves of his coal black, naturally curly hair could be seen. They all stood together so Janice could take several group pictures.

Jasmine told Shayna the colors James was wearing, so even though they weren't official dates, it appeared they were a couple for the prom. She chose an emerald green spaghetti strap, tea length gown that gathered at her small waist. Shayna chose a small brown purse and brown sandals as part of her ensemble. She accessorized her outfit with matching pearl earrings and necklace. She wore her hair down, letting it hang pass her shoulders, pulled back to one side with a hair comb with ivory roses attached to it. Everyone was happy as Janice took more pictures of them by the limo.

"Have fun and be safe," she said as they got into the car. Stephen and Jasmine sat next to each other. Shayna and James sat on the same seat, but left plenty of space between them. They talked about school and the upcoming graduation as they rode to the hotel.

The stretch white limo pulled up to the hotel. The driver got out and opened their door. When they got out they were treated like royalty. The first being the red carpet laid out for each person as they walked up to the hotel lobby. As they approached the room where their prom was being held, each guy was given a rose to present to a lady friend or pin to his lapel. Jasmine embraced Stephen when he gave her the beautiful red rose. Shayna's smile went all the way down to her heart when James presented her with his rose.

The prom was wonderful. Natalia joined their group and hung out with them for a while. When the music for a slow dance came on, Stephen and Jasmine left the other three standing on the side of the dance floor. James felt self-conscious, because he didn't know which girl to ask to dance. His problem was solved rather quickly when another classmate asked Natalia to dance.

James took Shayna by the hand. "Would you like to dance?" he asked politely.

She went with him to the dance floor. James held her tightly, but gently. Shayna felt special. She felt pretty.

"Shayna." James said her name softly.

"Yes?" she answered.

"You look very beautiful."

"Thank you, James," she replied and put her arm tighter around him.

They danced both slow songs and went for something to drink after the second song ended.

When it came time to take their prom pictures, Stephen and Jasmine took several poses together.

Shayna only had enough money to pay for a single pose, so she was done quickly. She was standing near the dance floor again watching her classmates when James touched her on the shoulder. She turned. When she saw who it was, she smiled.

"What can I do for you?" Shayna asked.

"You can take pictures with me," he said.

"Are you sure? Prom pictures are supposed to be special," she replied.

"I know. That's why I don't want to take mine alone." He smiled at her. "Besides, Jasmine went through a lot of trouble to get us to dress in the same colors."

They both laughed as the photographer called his number.

After the prom they all hung out at the burger place.

"It's after 3:00 am. We better head home," James said.

As excited as they all were, they were also very tired. The limo dropped Stephen and Shayna off and then the twins. Janice talked to them for a minute before she went to bed.

"I saw you hitting it off with Shayna," Jasmine teased her brother.

"She's nice. I don't like her crowd, but I do like her," he said.

"I can say the same about you and Stephen." Jasmine laughed. "Well, he doesn't have a crowd, but I really do like him."

They stood quiet for a moment and smiled at each other.

"James, Mama and Daddy would be very proud of us right now," Jasmine said.

"Yes they would, sis. Yes they would."

They shared a hug and went into their rooms.

●●●●●●●

Graduation came and went, and everyone started making plans for the summer. The twins and Shayna received full scholarships to the university. Stephen received a partial scholarship, so he knew he had to work over the summer to help pay his way through college. He and Jasmine made it official that they were a couple.

James and Shayna spent a lot of time together volunteering at the center. She got a part time job because she knew her cousin wasn't going to help her with any extra expenses. As all three were ending their time in grief counseling, Cherralyn told them her door was always open when they needed to talk.

Stephen finally got Jasmine to go to church. Each Sunday he was off from work, they went together. One Sunday Pastor Jones asked James and Jasmine to sing *His Eye Is On The Sparrow*. Jasmine had not sung in church in a long time. She was nervous until she stepped in front of the microphone.

Janice cried as she watched and listened to them sing. Stephen and Shayna thought their friends' voices sounded like they were flowing down from heaven.

●●●●●●●

Shayna was busy at work when she looked up and saw Michael coming towards her.

"I need to talk to you!" he said loudly.

Shayna saw everyone staring at her, including her boss. "You'll have to wait until I get off work. I can't talk to you now," she told him.

"Why, are you ashamed of me? You don't want these good people to know you've been with me?" he said angrily.

Before Shayna could say anything else, Michael grabbed her. "Come talk to me, I said!"

Shayna was crying. "Let go of me, Michael! I told you it's over between us."

Two security officers walked up. "Sir, if you don't let her go right now, we will have to arrest you."

Michael pushed Shayna away. "You ain't worth it! Your cousin treats you like trash, because you are trash!" He stormed out of the door.

"Are you okay, ma'am?" the officers asked her.

"Yes, thank you," Shayna replied and went to the restroom to wash her face, so she could get back to work.

Shayna's boss let her finish the shift and told her to take a few days off so she could take care of the problem that occurred earlier.

"Yes sir," was all she said and left.

●●●●●●●

When Shayna got to church that Sunday, a few of the members didn't speak to her. They stared and whispered about her during service. She remembered seeing a few of the ladies at her job when Michael caused that scene.

When Shayna got home, Latoya was livid.

"You've been sleeping with a low life like that? What kind of tramp are you Shayna? Did you bring him into my house?" she screamed. "I give you a roof over your head, and this is the way you repay me? You drag our good name into the dirt!"

"That's enough Latoya!" Richard cut in. "Stop screaming at her, like she's a child."

"An ungrateful child, that's what she is!" Latoya said, still angry.

Shayna stood up and approached her cousin. "You treat me like an outcast! How dare you call this a roof over my head, when you make me sleep in the garage? You think you're so high and mighty, cuz you live off of Richard's money!

"You won't let me cook in your precious kitchen or eat at your fancy table! I can't invite my friends over, and you think you're doing me a favor? I know you got the money from my mother's insurance policy to help take care of me, but you won't give me a dime!"

Tears ran down Shayna's face.

"You have the nerve to talk about me. You sit in church with the hypocrite section that looks down their noses at people. You are a hypocritical sleaze bag! If you would have listened when I tried to talk to you, maybe I wouldn't have ended up with Michael!" Shayna's words left Latoya speechless.

"You make me sick, Latoya!" Shayna turned and walked out.

Latoya's problems were just beginning, as Richard looked at her in disgust. "Right now you make me sick, too," he said and walked out of the front door.

●●●●●●●

The following day, Shayna sat in her car in front of the center and prayed. *Lord, who can I go to for help? Please God, guide me. I need help. Amen.*

Shayna knew she needed a job, because now she would need somewhere to stay until school started in the fall, and she could live in the dorm at the university.

She knocked on the door of Cherralyn's office.

"Come in," she said. "Hi, Shayna. What can I do for you?"

"I need to talk to you," Shayna replied.

"Have a seat." Cherralyn pointed to one of the seats in front of her desk.

Shayna sat down and dropped her head. Cherralyn was at the restaurant when Michael showed up. She was coming out of the ladies room, and she mixed in with the crowd, so she knew Shayna hadn't seen her.

"Talk to me," Cherralyn said softly as she got up from her desk and went to sit next to her.

Through tears, Shayna told her everything. "That's the truth, Ms. Cherralyn. I promise," she said still crying.

"We do need someone part time to help put away supplies and to help clean the classrooms. Are you willing to take that job?" Cherralyn asked.

"Yes, ma'am. Thank you," Shayna said, seeing a little light at the end of the tunnel.

"Since you volunteer in the mornings, would you like to make that your clock in time?"

Shayna looked at Cherralyn. "Thank you for being so nice, but I would like to continue volunteering in the morning and work in the evening." Shayna knew that would keep her busy and off the street during the day.

"That's fine, Shayna. I'll send Melanie over to the Welcoming Center, so you can fill out the proper paper work."

They both stood up. Cherralyn held her in a caring embrace for a moment. "Welcome to our staff at The Bracie Shaw Outreach Center," she said smiling.

Shayna hugged Cherralyn and then went to catch Melanie, to make things official.

Chapter 6

Jasmine was spending a lot of time with Stephen. They were sitting at the burger place when Stephen told her his family would be moving.

"We're not going far, about 45 minutes away. I already have a job lined-up," he said.

"What about us?" Jasmine asked.

"We're still a couple. I'll be at the university in the fall, and I'm not changing my church membership. Every Sunday I have off work, I'll be here for service," he said, trying to comfort her.

"When are you moving?" she asked.

"We've already started. My dad started his new job there, but my mom will still be working for Mrs. Davenport. Jasmine, we will finally be living in our own place," he said.

Stephen and his parents had been living in the Davenport's guest home for over three years. Because his mother worked for the Davenports, Stephen's parents enrolled him in school using their address. Everyone at school thought the house belonged to his family. The Davenports didn't charge much for rent, so his parents were able to save for their own home. It was Mrs. Davenport who told his family about God's plan of salvation, and she lived it every day.

Stephen and his family had been in their new home for a few weeks when he invited Jasmine over to see it. She told James and her aunt that she would be spending the night at Shayna's, so they wouldn't know she was spending it at Stephen's.

"My parents are gone for the weekend so it'll be ok for you to stay the night," Stephen said as he and Jasmine walked through the front door of his new home.

"The lawn is beautiful, now give me a tour of the house," she said smiling.

As Stephen showed her around she could see the pride on his face. They went into the kitchen and made dinner. They sat at the table and talked while they ate.

"It's getting late, are you ready for bed?" he asked when they were done.

"Yes," she answered.

They cleaned the kitchen, then Stephen showed her to the guest room.

"Everything you need is in the connecting restroom. Sleep good, and I'll see you in the morning."

"Thank you," Jasmine said. Stephen kissed her on the head and closed the door.

Jasmine showered and dressed for bed. She brushed her hair into a ponytail and sat on the side of the bed. She wasn't as sleepy as she thought. Stephen was in the room next door. He showered and put on his pajamas. Stephen knew he was in love with Jasmine when he served her that first order of fries and a medium fruit drink. He had already made up his mind to go to college, so he could provide for her. Stephen knew he wanted to marry her someday.

A knock on the door brought Stephen out of his thoughts. "Come in," he said.

Jasmine stepped inside his door and closed it. Stephen was speechless at her beauty as she walked over to him. He stood up and kissed her.

"You are beautiful Jasmine," he said in almost a whisper.

"Thank you."

"Are you sure you want to do this?" he asked her.

"With you Stephen, yes. I love you."

"I love you, too, Jasmine."

●●●●●●●

The following week, Jasmine seemed to be on a cloud. She hummed and danced around the house a lot. Janice watched her niece. *She's not a virgin anymore,* she thought to herself. Janice remembered the humming and dancing from her own youth. Now she had to figure out how to talk to her niece about protection.

●●●●●●●

Cherralyn called Shayna into her office. "Close the door and have a seat," she said.

Shayna was nervous. Life finally seemed to be working out for her. She tried to think of something she may have done wrong.

"You have been doing an excellent job these past few weeks. Our six and seven-year-olds' summer class is getting larger, and I wondered if you would like to help an extra two hours each day with arts and crafts? You will be getting paid for that time," Cherralyn said.

"I would love to," Shayna said, wiping tears from her eyes. "Thank you Ms. Cherralyn. I thought I did something wrong. I am trying so hard now to be the young lady my mother taught me to be."

Cherralyn walked over to her. "I'm very proud of you, Shayna. Change takes courage and determination. I see you have both."

Cherralyn thought about Bracie's talks with her and lifted Shayna's chin. "You must change and do better for you. Remember everything your mother taught you. Let the Bible be your standard, and you won't go wrong. Move forward for Shayna, and don't let people's opinions sway you from getting better."

"Yes, ma'am," she said and left the office happy.

Shayna was humming as she walked down the hall of the center. She turned the corner and bumped into James.

"So that was your lovely voice I heard."

Shayna looked around. "Me?" she asked, truly surprised by his words.

"You're the only one standing here," James said.

"Well thank you," she said and started to walk off.

"Shayna, would you like to go out with me?'" James asked nervously. "On a date?"

"Yes, I would like that." She went into the classroom smiling. This day just keeps getting better, she thought.

Chapter 7

"Where is she?" Richard yelled at Latoya.

"I don't know. I've tried her cell, but she won't answer," Latoya said with her head down.

"Can you blame her, after the way you treated her! She loved you Latoya, and she looked up to you. When she needed you most, you could only think of yourself!" he continued to yell at her.

"I'm sorry Richard. I don't know what else to say." When she tried to touch him, Richard moved away from her. "Find her! She doesn't need to be in the streets in the state of mind she was in."

Richard looked at his wife and slammed the door of the guest room where he had been sleeping since their family blowup a few weeks earlier.

Latoya sat at the table, and for the first time in years she sincerely prayed to God. *"Father, first I ask you to forgive me for sinning against you. You blessed my husband, and I used it for my own personal gain. I wanted status more than I wanted your favor. Please forgive me. Father, please let my cousin be safe. I promise if you bring her home, I will be a better person. Father, please help me fix my marriage. I love Richard, and I don't want to lose him. Amen."*

Latoya put her head on the table and cried. Richard could hear her down the hall. He walked into the kitchen and touched her on the shoulder.

"I am so sorry, Richard. If anything happens to her, I'll never forgive myself."

"Let's go try to find her," he said.

Latoya dried her face as they got into the car to go look for her cousin.

They went to the Harpers' home. Janice opened the door. "May I help you?"

"Hi, my name is Latoya, and I'm looking for my cousin Shayna."

Janice smiled, "She left a few minutes ago with James and Jasmine."

Latoya felt relieved. "Do you know when they'll be back?" she asked.

"Not until later. They went to the Outreach Center," Janice told her.

"Thank you, and it was nice to meet you," Latoya said and left.

Richard and Latoya went into the center together. Melanie greeted them. She asked the couple to follow her as she led them into the office. When Cherralyn told them to come in, Melanie introduced them and left.

"How may I help you?" Cherralyn told them as she signaled for them to have a seat. Latoya started talking first. She told the truth, even though she knew Richard might become angry again.

"She does volunteer and work here," Cherralyn said. "She's a wonderful young lady."

Latoya and Richard smiled.

"Did you know she received a full scholarship with room and board at the university?" Cherralyn asked both of them.

They both felt ashamed, Latoya for lying and not caring and Richard for not standing up to his wife and talking to Shayna himself.

"I didn't see you at her graduation," Cherralyn said. "She graduated in the top five percent of her class."

Richard was upset because he later found out his wife had purposely booked their trip to Jamaica that weekend without telling him about the graduation.

Latoya dropped her head and said, "We were out of town."

"Well she's gone for the evening. A lot of the youth went to the movies," Cherralyn said, annoyed with her.

Richard stood up and shook her hand again. "Thank you. Will you tell her to call me on my phone when you see her again? Thank you for watching out for her," he said. Richard opened the door for his wife and they left.

Back at home, Richard stood in the kitchen while Latoya sat at the table.

"Did you remember to thank Ms. Harper for letting Shayna stay there?"

Latoya started to lie and say yes, but she was already in enough trouble. "No, I only said it was nice to meet her because I wanted to hurry and get to the center," she sat there with her head down.

Richard walked around the table and touched her on the shoulder. "I understand. We'll go over there tomorrow. I'm going to bed. Goodnight."

He left her sitting there as he went back to the guestroom. Tears ran down Latoya's face as she heard the lock click on his door. She thought her husband would be sleeping in their bed tonight. She was wrong.

●●●●●●●

Cherralyn returned to the center later that night. She looked at her watch. It was several hours past closing. *Whose car is that*, she wondered? It looked familiar, but she wasn't taking any chances. She called the security company and told them about the car. A few minutes later, the security arrived, and they pulled into the driveway together.

Cherralyn stayed in her vehicle while the officers approached the parked car. She was shocked when Shayna stepped out of the car. "I know her," she said to the officers as she headed in their direction.

They all went into the center. While the officers looked around, Cherralyn called her husband, so he would not be worried about her. She also called Richard, who said he was on his way.

"I can explain," Shayna said.

"There is no need, just sit there please," Cherralyn replied softly. There was a knock on the front door. "Wait here." Cherralyn walked away, she came back with Richard.

"Shayna!" He was relieved to see that she was okay. Richard grabbed her and held her tightly. She didn't say anything. "Can I talk to her alone?" he asked.

Cherralyn went to her office to get the papers she had come back for. Richard and Shayna talked for the first time. On the way out they thanked Cherralyn for calling him. Shayna followed Richard to the house.

●●●●●●●

Later that week, Jasmine was happy as she walked into the center. In the last month she had been able to spend a few nights with Stephen. Getting away from the house had been easier than she thought. Now she had to talk to Shayna, so they could get their story together. She didn't want Shayna to accidently tell James she had not being staying at her house.

Before she could find Shayna Cherralyn called her into her office. "How are you doing? I haven't seen you since graduation."

"I'm doing fine. I've been keeping busy, that's all," Jasmine answered.

"How are things at home?" Cherralyn asked.

"What do you mean?" Jasmine asked defensively. "I'm not doing anything!"

Cherralyn looked at Jasmine. She knew the reason for Jasmine's being so defensive, because Janice had already come to her for advice. "Are you thinking about becoming sexually active, Jasmine?" she asked, hoping not to give away the fact that she already knew she had.

"I don't think that's any of your business!" she replied.

"I just want you to be careful. You could get pregnant or..." Before Cherralyn could finish her sentence, Jasmine cut her off.

"I won't!" she said very rudely.

Cherralyn stood in front of her. "There are a lot of things out there that are worse than getting pregnant, if you're not careful."

"Are you trying to say I'm sleeping around?" Jasmine yelled.

"No, Jasmine, but your partner might be."

"He's not!" Jasmine answered, very rudely again.

Cherralyn took Jasmine by the hand and tried to ease the tension between them. "Jasmine, I care and I only want what's best for you. You have a full scholarship to college, and I don't want you to mess that up," she said calmly.

Jasmine pulled her hand from Cherralyn's grasp. "I don't need you to be concerned about me. I only came to this center because of my aunt and my brother. I'm kinda tired of everyone thinking they know what's best for me. Tell Shayna I came by looking for her!" Jasmine rolled her eyes at Cherralyn and slammed the door on her way out of the office.

•••••••

Richard and Latoya knocked on the Harper's door. Janice smiled when she saw the couple.

"Hello, it's nice to see you again. But Shayna isn't here."

"We know. We wanted to thank you for letting her stay here when she was away from home."

Janice looked at them confused. "I don't know what you're talking about. Please come in."

James' door was cracked, and he heard their entire conversation. Where had Jasmine been? Apparently she had been lying for over a month about staying at Shayna's. He left out the back and went to the center.

"What's wrong James?" Cherralyn asked as soon as he stepped through the door.

James didn't realize tears were running down his face. "Jasmine's been lying about staying at Shayna's. She has been staying out doing who knows what with God knows who. I can't believe she's doing this. Our aunt has been so kind to us," he said trying to be strong.

Cherralyn took James to her office so she could talk with him.

●●●●●●●

Later that day, Jasmine returned to the house and headed for her room. Janice called her to the den.

"Where have you been?" she asked trying to remain calm.

Jasmine knew something was wrong from her aunt's tone of voice. "With my friends," she answered nonchalantly.

"Where have you been spending nights this past month?" Janice asked, her calmness slipping away.

Jasmine stood speechless.

"Before you say anything, I know you have not been staying at Shayna's." "So where have you been, and who have you been staying with?" Janice was visibly upset.

"I don't have to tell you anything!" Jasmine yelled.

"As long as you live in this house, you have to let me know where you are and who you're with," Janice replied sternly.

"You're not my mother! I don't owe you an explanation for where I am or who I'm with!"

"Yes you do!" Janice replied.

"No I don't!"

Janice's next statement angered Jasmine even more. "You think because you're having sex now, that you're grown!"

Jasmine glared at her aunt. "That is none of your business! Why is everyone in my business? I am grown, and I am going to college to be on my own!"

"That doesn't make you grown, Jasmine. You need to slow down and think. You should not be sleeping with some boy who is not your husband," Janice told her.

"I don't have to take this!" Jasmine yelled and turned to walk away.

"Don't walk away from me, young lady." Janice grabbed her niece's arm.

Jasmine turned and back-handed her aunt across the face. Before she could recover from the blow, Jasmine hit Janice in the chest and knocked her to the floor. Janice looked up at her niece in shock.

"Oh my God, what have I done?" Jasmine said as she ran out of the house.

When James returned, he saw the bruise on Janice's face, and he knew he was too late. "She hit you?!" he said in shock.

Janice only nodded. James could tell she had been crying. Janice moved the ice pack from her chest and James noticed the bruise that was there.

"Did she hit you or kick you?" he asked softly.

Janice looked up at him surprised by his question. "She hit me," she answered in barely a whisper.

"We're both fully trained in martial arts. We are black belts, Auntie. Jasmine could have really hurt you. She knows better than to react in anger." James was angry and ashamed that his sister would hurt their aunt.

"It's not your fault, son. Jasmine has to work out her own problems. I love her, but she needs more help than I can give her." Janice picked up the ice pack and went to her room.

Chapter 8

Jasmine told Stephen what happened with her aunt. "I don't know what to say," she said. "I feel so bad."

"You have to apologize to her," he said. Stephen tried to get Jasmine to call her family, but to no avail. She had been with him since she left her aunt's house earlier that day, but his parents were coming home soon.

"I can't go back now. Everyone is still so angry with me. I don't have anywhere else to go," she started to cry.

"Don't cry. I know where you can stay for a while. Follow me in your car."

They drove for over an hour. Jasmine followed Stephen into the driveway of a beautiful home. He opened her door and they walked up to the front door and rang the bell.

"Hey cuz," a middle aged woman gave him a big hug when she answered the door. He introduced Jasmine to his cousin Claudia.

"Can she stay here with you for a while?" he asked her. Both ladies turned to look at him. "Just until school starts? She has a scholarship to live in the dorms." Stephen looked at his cousin, waiting for her to answer.

"Where are your parents?" Claudia asked.

Jasmine turned to her. "They were killed in a car accident almost a year ago. I was living with my aunt, but it's not working out so well," she said with tears in her eyes.

Claudia told them it would be okay, but only until school started.

"Thank you," Jasmine said.

Claudia showed Jasmine to her room and told Stephen to take the other guestroom for the night. "You can't sleep together in my home when you are not married."

"I understand," Jasmine answered.

"It doesn't matter if you understand it or not. It's my home and my rule," she replied.

Later they all ate dinner together and engaged in general conversation. And then everyone showered and got ready for bed.

"You're going to be okay here," Stephen assured Jasmine. He kissed her goodnight and they went into their separate rooms.

•••••••

Stephen spent the next day showing Jasmine around. When he had to leave, Jasmine went into her room and cried. Claudia heard her, but she let her be.

Jasmine's phone rang. "Hey brother, I'm okay. Did I hurt Aunt Janice? I am so sorry James. She grabbed me, and I reacted. I would never purposely hurt her." Jasmine started crying again.

Jasmine where are you? Tell me where you are so I can come and get you." Jasmine sat quietly for a moment.

"You can't come get me," she spoke softly.

"Why? Are you ok? Are you in some sort of trouble?"

"Not like you're thinking. I'm okay, I promise."

"Please let me come get you. I don't know what I'll do if something happens to you. Please, Jasmine," James begged. She sat quietly again. She wasn't prepared for the hurt and agony she could hear in her brother's voice. Jasmine put her hand over her stomach. She took a deep breath, and with tears streaming down her face she told him, "I can't come back, James, not right now. I'm staying with a friend. Try not to worry about me. Where I am there's an adult, so I'll be ok. "

"But, you need to..."

"I'll stay in touch. I love you." Jasmine hung up the phone. When she finally laid down, sleep came crashing down upon her.

●●●●●●●

Claudia and Jasmine got along fine. They talked a lot. Jasmine told her the truth about everything that happened. Claudia sat and listened.

"Do you feel better with all of that off your shoulders?"

"Yes, ma'am," Jasmine answered.

"You need to call your aunt and apologize and let her know you're okay."

"Yes, ma'am," she answered again. She would call her aunt soon, she just didn't know when.

A week passed before Stephen came to see her again. They spent all of their time together except at night. They walked out to his cousin's fruit trees and sat on one of the benches.

"It smells so good out here, and it's so beautiful," Jasmine said. "What am I going to do about school? I need to turn in the last of my paperwork."

"Give me all your papers, and I'll turn them in for you," he said. When Stephen got ready to leave, he made sure she had given him all of her papers for school.

Claudia had been keeping a close eye on Jasmine. She was tired most of the time, even though she slept a lot, and she was not keeping most of her food down. One afternoon she called Jasmine out to the garden bench.

"Sit down." Jasmine sat there fidgeting with her hands, thinking Claudia was going to tell her to leave.

"Do you realize you're pregnant?" Claudia asked her.

"No, ma'am, I can't be," she said.

"Have you ever slept with my cousin?"

Jasmine dropped her head and answered her. "Yes, ma'am, but only a few times."

Claudia looked at Jasmine and lifted her head so she could see her face. "Well, my dear, it only takes once. Since you chose to have sex, why didn't you use protection? You and Stephen were very irresponsible."

Jasmine dropped her head again.

"You need to talk to Stephen, and you'll need to see a doctor. Do you realize you have a great responsibility before you?"

"Yes, ma'am," was all Jasmine said and went into the house. She lay in bed staring at the ceiling. *"Pregnant? Lord, what am I going to do?"* she asked softly.

A few days later Jasmine heard Claudia talking to Stephen on the phone. She was excited to know he would be visiting soon. When he arrived, he and Jasmine went and sat in the garden. He held her hand as they sat quietly listening to the wind blowing in the trees.

"I turned in your papers for school," he finally said. Jasmine gave him a little smile. "I thought you would be more excited than that," he said.

She squeezed his hand. "Stephen, let's not go to college here. We can move somewhere else," she said.

He turned and looked at her. "You're kidding, right?"

Jasmine looked at him. "No. We can get married, have a family, and go to college somewhere else," she said, hoping he would agree.

"I love you, but I want to go to college here," he said. "Besides, I have a partial scholarship that I can't afford to give up."

Jasmine dropped her head. She couldn't tell him about the pregnancy test that came back positive. "You're right," she said. "I was being silly. I'll be ready to go back to Aunt Janice soon, so I can get my things ready for school."

Stephen was glad she came to her senses. He stood, kissed her and went into the house.

Chapter 9

Jasmine wasn't shocked that Stephen didn't want to get married. *Now what?* she thought. She lay in bed trying to wrap her mind around what was happening to her. *Disrespect is sin.* She kept hearing her mother's voice in her head. *Okay, I will fix it,* she said to herself as she dozed off to sleep.

•••••••

Claudia came into the house from work and saw a note left by Jasmine: *Ms. Claudia, thank you for your wonderful hospitality. I know I have some major decisions to make. I have decided to have an abortion and go home. Raising a baby will be too much while going to school. Stephen nor I are ready to be responsible for another life. Please keep me in your prayers. Sincerely, Jasmine Harper.*

Claudia put the note down and called Stephen.

Stephen was at his cousin's home by nightfall. Once he took a seat, she gave him the note. He read the note and dropped his head. Claudia touched his shoulder.

"I did say we weren't ready to get married or have a family. But I didn't know she was already pregnant." Tears ran down his face. "God is punishing me for having sex out of marriage," he said with his head still down.

"That's foolish Stephen. You know God does not work like that. He is a forgiving God. Don't blame him for y'all's mistakes," she told him sternly, but with compassion.

"Yes, ma'am, I do know better. It just hurts to know she would do this to my child, especially without my knowledge," he said as tears continued to flow down his face.

"Go to bed son, and maybe you can talk to her tomorrow."

Stephen showered and went to bed without eating. Sleep did not come easy for him.

● ● ● ● ● ● ●

The first week of school came and went. Stephen saw no signs of Jasmine. He figured she was still upset about the baby and was avoiding him. James went to a few of the classes he knew his sister should be taking. He had not seen her either.

One Saturday afternoon, Stephen knocked on the Harper's door.

"Hello, Stephen, come in." Janice stepped aside to allow him entry. When she closed the door, she called for James.

By the time he reached the den, Stephen said he had come to see Jasmine. They both looked at him strangely.

"She's been gone for over a month now," James said. Stephen stood there with confusion on his face now. Janice walked over to him.

"What do you know, Stephen? What are you not telling us?" she asked.

Stephen told them Jasmine had been staying with his cousin since she left home. "She said she was coming home, but that was two weeks ago," he said concerned.

James grabbed Stephen and started to choke him. "You knew we were looking for her, and you never said anything!" he shouted.

Stephen pushed him away. "I knew she was safe, and she was trying to give your aunt time to cool off. I heard her talking with you, and I assumed she told you," he said.

"You should have made sure I knew!" James yelled as he went after Stephen again.

"Stop it, both of you!" Janice said firmly. "What did she tell you Stephen?" she asked more calmly than she was feeling.

"Only that she was coming home to get ready for school."

"I have not seen her at school," James said.

"Me neither," said Stephen. "That's why I came here looking for her." He decided not to mention the pregnancy or the abortion, knowing it would make them more upset.

●●●●●●●

While James confronted Stephen, Jasmine was at the Outreach Center looking for her brother. Cherralyn greeted her as she walked in the door. The two hugged and went into her office.

"How have you been? I've missed you," Cherralyn told her.

"I'm fine, just taking it day by day," Jasmine replied. "Is James here? I need to talk to him," she said.

"No, he's off today."

"Okay, thank you," Jasmine said as she started to get up from her chair. But then she sat back down. "Ms. Cherralyn, please forgive me for being so disrespectful the last time I was here. I should have listened," she said as tears welled up in her eyes.

Cherralyn looked at her and smiled. "Apology accepted." She leaned forward in her chair. "Jasmine, have you talked with your aunt?"

"No, ma'am," she answered.

"You need to. Baby, we all make mistakes. But you have to be grown up enough to say I'm sorry. Your aunt loves you."

She sat there knowing Cherralyn was telling her right, but still felt she couldn't go back, not now. "I'll call her," she said.

"Jasmine, always remember God is only a prayer away. He's waiting on you. He will not force His will upon you."

Jasmine started crying. "Why did God take my parents, Ms. Cherralyn? If He loves me so much, why does He let this pain bear down on me?"

Cherralyn walked from behind her desk and held Jasmine in her arms. "God does love you Jasmine, but this world's pain will come. You know everyone that is born will one day die. It's His Word. It's a promise."

"I know, but I wasn't ready to lose my parents," she said through her tears.

"I know baby. Death does take us by surprise sometimes. It hurts, but we still have to go on, and we still have to live," she said comforting Jasmine. "When you miss your parents, it's okay to cry." Cherralyn shared something Bracie had always told her: "Remember, tears cried in faith gives you strength to go on."

"Thank you, Ms. Cherralyn. I needed to talk to you. I do feel better now. I will call James and my aunt," she said.

Cherralyn embraced Jasmine again and walked her to the door. "Call me whenever you need to talk."

●●●●●●●

Once everyone was gone for the evening, Cherralyn stood in the Welcoming Center looking at the portrait of Tyler and Bracie. Her husband David walked up behind her and wrapped her in his arms.

"What's on your mind?" he asked.

Cherralyn leaned back into his embrace. "I didn't realize running the center would have me involved in the lives of so many young people," she said.

"Is it too much for you?"

"No, I just hope I'm doing a good job," she replied. "Bracie seemed to know how to handle every situation that came through the door."

David turned his wife towards him. "You pray every morning, and I know you're praying throughout the day. So you are not alone. You're doing a wonderful job, but you must always leave room for God to work," he said while he caressed her face. "The youth here look up to you, Cherralyn. They trust you."

"I know, and I want to make sure I'm leading them right," she said.

"And you are," David said as he took his wife by the hand. "You had an excellent mentor. Now let's go home."

Later that evening, the couple was finishing dinner when the gate buzzer rang. They opened the door and Carl and Shanelle stepped into the foyer. Shanelle took a deep breath as she walked into the sitting room. Tyler and Bracie had made the decision to leave the house for Cherralyn and it was her first time there since she and Carl had removed all of Tyler and Bracie's personal items from the home. Carl and Shanelle were the closest people in Tyler's and later Bracie's life, more than best friends, but family.

"Are you okay?" Carl asked her softly.

"Yes," Shanelle answered as she looked around the room.

Carl placed a box on the table. "Bracie's children sent these four scrapbooks back. They ask that you keep one and put the other three in the Welcoming Center."

Cherralyn looked at the books. She remembered the long hours Bracie spent on making them. She was touched by the generosity of Bracie's children.

"Will you tell them thank you?" she asked.

"Sure," Carl answered.

"Ms. Shanelle?" Cherralyn called her name softly.

Shanelle looked at her.

"Do you think Ms. Bracie would mind if I change the guestroom next to the master suite into a nursery?" she asked smiling.

David looked at his wife surprised. "You mean like a baby nursery?"

Cherralyn nodded while laughing at her husband.

"I'm going to be a daddy!" he said excited.

Carl and Shanell hugged the couple and congratulated them.

"Can you go upstairs with me for a minute?" asked Cherralyn.

Both ladies went upstairs and left the men downstairs talking. Shanelle looked around as they walked up the stairs.

"You seem to have left everything like it was," she said.

"Ms. Bracie's home was already beautiful. I just added some of our personal things," she answered.

Shanelle and Cherralyn began working on design plans for the nursery. They didn't realize two hours had passed until Carl called for his wife.

"It's time to go, Shanelle. We have to pick up our son."

"Okay we're on the way down," she replied.

David and Cherralyn walked them to the door.

"Thanks for helping me," Cherralyn said.

"Anytime, and Cherralyn..."

"Yes, Ms. Shanelle?"

"Please stop referring to this as Bracie's home. It is yours and David's now."

The couple looked at both her and Carl.

"We won't be offended. We have no reason to be," Shanelle said. "This is your home now. You can do with it as you please."

Shanelle hugged her again. She knew Cherralyn needed to hear that from her, so she could embrace the home as her own.

A few days later, Cherralyn sat at her desk thinking about the visit with Carl and Shanelle. When she asked Shanelle about the bedroom furniture, she simply said, "Do what you think Bracie would have done with it."

A knock on the door interrupted her thoughts. Melanie walked in and sat down.

"How is the new house coming along?" Cherralyn asked her.

"I love it!" Melanie said excited.

"That's why I asked you in. The bedroom set that you like from Bracie's, I mean my home, I would like for you to have it."

Melanie sat there speechless. She fell in love with that bedroom set the first time Bracie invited her over, and she slept there each time she visited.

Cherralyn gave her a card. "Call the movers and set up a time that is best for you."

"Thank you!" Melanie hugged her and went to call her husband.

Cherralyn smiled. She was glad Melanie was happy. She knew in her heart Bracie would want her to have the furniture that was so special to her.

Chapter 10

Jasmine sat on the bed of the tiny room she rented. *My credit card is maxed-out, but my rent is paid for five months*, she thought to herself. James kept the cell phone bills paid, so that was one less thing she had to worry about.

Jasmine brought along the clothes Claudia had given her. Some of them were a little large on her. She figured the clothes would come in handy when she started getting bigger with the pregnancy. *How did I get myself into this mess?* she asked herself. She was startled when she answered the question herself, *DISOBEDIENCE and DISRESPECT!*

It was a beautiful day outside, so Jasmine walked to the park and sat on a bench. She watched the children as they ran and played on the playground equipment. She touched her stomach as it grumbled from hunger. She pulled the cheese crackers and milk from her bag. Jasmine didn't care much for the crackers, but right now they tasted like heaven.

She continued to watch the children as they played. Jasmine noticed a little girl about five years old walking towards her. The little girl sat next to her and smiled. Jasmine smiled back, but didn't say anything.

"Hi, my name is Kaylin. I like crackers, too," the child said through her smile.

Jasmine looked down at her lunch and shared one of the crackers. By the time Kaylin bit into the cracker, her mom was standing in front of them.

"I'm sorry," she said to Jasmine. "Kaylin, you know better!"

"It's okay," Jasmine said. "I was glad to share with her, so I wouldn't have to eat alone."

"Can I sit here, Mama?" Kaylin asked, looking at Jasmine.

"It's okay with me, I'm not leaving anytime soon," Jasmine told the mother.

"I'll be a few steps away," her mother said.

"What's your name?" Kaylin asked.

"My name is Jasmine."

"That's a pretty name."

"So is Kaylin," Jasmine replied.

They talked about flowers and other things in the park. Kaylin told Jasmine about her favorite cartoons and her dolls. Kaylin's mother let them talk for about ten minutes before she walked back to the bench where they sat.

"It's time to go, sweetie. Tell the nice lady goodbye."

"Her name is Ms. Jasmine, Mama, and she likes flowers," Kaylin said.

"Okay." She smiled at Jasmine and then her daughter. "It's nice to meet you, Jasmine," she said as she took Kaylin by the hand.

Jasmine watched them walk away, as Kaylin talked nonstop. *That will be me in a few more years*, Jasmine laughed to herself.

●●●●●●●

Latoya had been seeking God with her heart but didn't know where to start. She sat in front of the church in her car and prayed. *"Lord, I thank you for giving me another opportunity to talk to you. Lord, I need you to come into my home. I need to know how to fix the relationships that I have torn apart.*

"Lord, please tell me how to mend my relationship with my cousin, and help me restore my husband's trust in me. Save my family, Lord. Save me," she cried. *"Lord, who can I talk to? Where can I go to get help?"* Latoya said, *"Amen,"* and drove out of the parking lot.

Later, she found herself at the Outreach Center. She knew being here had helped Shayna. She stood looking at the portrait of Tyler and Bracie when Cherralyn touched her on the shoulder.

"They were a very beautiful couple," she said.

"Yes, they were," Cherralyn agreed. "How may I help you?"

"I prayed for guidance, and I ended up here," Latoya answered.

Cherralyn and Latoya went into her office. She sat silently as tears filled her eyes. Cherralyn sat next to her.

"Talk to me," she said.

Latoya told how she had lost track of who she was and how ugly her heart became when Richard inherited his grandfather's estate. She told how she had treated Shayna and how it led to her running away. She was honest with Cherralyn about how she had lied and purposely hid things from Richard. She told how he had become very disappointed in her.

"He still sleeps in the guestroom, and I want my husband back," she said, sobbing.

Cherralyn touched her hand and silently asked God to be with her as she talked to Latoya.

"First you must ask God to forgive you," Cherralyn said.

"I have over and over again," she replied.

"Now you have to forgive yourself, and ask your family for forgiveness."

"I told them I was sorry," Latoya said.

"Sorry for what?" Cherralyn asked.

"For what I did," she replied.

"And what did you do?" Cherralyn asked her.

Latoya looked up at her confused. "I just told you," she said.

"You need to tell your family that. Right now they don't know if you're sorry for your actions or sorry that it all caught up with you."

"I understand," she said.

Cherralyn walked Latoya back to the Welcoming Center. She prayed with her and watched her leave.

"Father, please restore her family," she prayed and went back to her office.

Latoya went home and called her family into the kitchen. She poured from her heart what she did and why she did it. Latoya apologized to Richard and Shayna. They walked around the table and hugged her.

"We accept your apology," they said at once.

"Now we can start healing, and our house can become a Godly HOME," Latoya said softly.

Richard prayed as they held hands as a family for the first time since Shayna had arrived.

Thank you Father, Latoya said to herself as she and Richard enjoyed the intimacy of being husband and wife again.

Chapter 11

Jasmine stood inside the foyer of the church waiting as the usher went to get James. She suddenly realized how much she missed coming, and now regretted waiting for so long to attend. Right now she needed some money, and she knew her brother would help her.

Two trustees walked out of the finance office and spoke to her on their way back into the santuary. Jasmine knew it would be a moment before James came outside, because he was in the choir, and they were still singing.

What if the usher gets Aunt Janice? I can't let her see me like this, Jasmine thought, and she started to panic. She still wasn't ready to face her aunt.

"Forgive me, Lord," she said as she kicked the door to the office open. Jasmine went inside and closed the door. She went to the cupboard and moved the statue of an angel. "Thank God they still put the money baskets here," she said. She remembered her Aunt Janice telling them they needed to get a better system for keeping the money safe until Monday's deposit. Now she was glad they had not taken her advice.

She took one of the baskets and started taking out the bills. *This is to slow*, she thought, as she heard the choir ending their song. Jasmine picked up a handful of the tithing envelopes and rushed out, making sure to close the door behind her.

●●●●●●●

Janice and James rushed out to find the foyer empty. Janice turned to the usher.

"Why didn't you get me?" she asked.

The usher shook her head. "I asked her, but she only wanted to see her brother."

"Okay, I understand," Janice sounded disappointed.

James could see the hurt on his aunt's face. They went back in together and enjoyed the rest of the service as best as they could.

Later that day, Janice, James and Shayna were eating dinner when the phone rang. Janice answered it.

"Yes, sir. No, sir. ARE YOU SERIOUS? JASMINE? Yes, sir, I'm on my way."

She hung up the phone and all three of them left. They dropped Shayna off at home.

"I'm praying for you," she said to James as she got out of the car.

Janice still had not said anything as they headed to the church. When they got there, James and Janice watched the surveillance video in disbelief. They all sat in silence for a moment.

"We found envelopes stacked neatly by the back door with a note saying she would pay it all back," said the trustee.

James looked at the note with Jasmine's signature on it. He gave it to his aunt as he confirmed the handwriting was hers.

"How much did she take?" he asked.

The trustee pulled out the record sheet they used earlier. "From the calculations here, she took $3,746."

Janice took out her check book and wrote out a check for $4,300. "The rest is to cover the cost of the door," she said.

Pastor Jones looked at Janice. He could tell she was embarrassed and angry, but more than that she was deeply hurt. He touched her shoulder. Janice acknowledged he was there, but couldn't look up.

"No one else knows about this, Sister Janice, and we plan to keep it that way. Because your niece signed her name to that note, she innocently admitted to theft. That was not a loan. She stole it," Pastor Jones said. "But, because you have been a faithful member here for such a long time, we will not press charges against her. Even though you have replaced what she has taken, you can no longer serve on the finance committee. You can submit your letter of resignation to the committee chair by Wednesday," he said with compassion.

"I understand and I will," Janice said with her head still down. She and James were walking towards the door when Pastor Jones stopped them.

"I'm sorry this happened. I'll be praying for you and your family. Sister Janice, all that has happened will not leave this office. That's a promise," he assured her.

"It all stays here," the trustee agreed, feeling sorry for her.

Later that evening, James got an unexpected call from his sister. "Girl, are you crazy?! What were you thinking? You stole from the church!"

Jasmine still had not realized she committed a crime. "Why are you so upset? I didn't steal anything. I left a note saying I would pay it back," she replied rather sharply.

James calmed down and explained everything to his sister. Jasmine sat on the side of the bed in shock.

"Please tell Aunt Janice I'm so sorry," she said in barely a whisper. "I didn't mean for this to happen. Auntie has served on that committee since we were children."

James could tell she was crying. "Come home, sis, so we can fix this and get things back to normal."

"There is no more normal for me. I keep messing up," Jasmine said through her tears.

"We all mess up, sis. But God still loves us, and so does our family."

Jasmine sat silently for a minute. "I don't know, bro. I have to work some things out, and then I'll see."

"Jasmine, Stephen is looking for you. He said you were coming home." James hoped that would make her change her mind and persuade her to return.

"Tell him hello." She quickly changed the subject. "How's Shayna?"

He was surprised she didn't say more about Stephen, but he answered her question.

"She's doing fine. She and her family are getting along really well now. We're dating. I really care about her."

"I'm glad. She's liked you for a while. I love you, James. I'll stay in touch." Jasmine hung up before he could say anything else.

He placed the phone on the counter. Janice was standing beside him. She touched his hand and told him to pray for Jasmine.

"That's all we can do for her right now." She embraced her nephew and went to her room to pray for her niece also.

●●●●●●●

Jasmine looked at the money on the table. *"Lord, I needed this money so I could pay for lights and water, and see the doctor. I wasn't stealing it. I promise I was going to find a way to pay it back. It was supposed to be a loan, that's why I left the note. I am so sorry, Lord,"* she said crying.

How do I keep doing everything wrong and making things worse? I can't go back, Jasmine thought to herself. She lay down and cried herself to sleep.

Chapter 12

Cherralyn and Shayna left the class of six year olds to go to the teen grief class. It was coming to an end when they walked in. Juliana was talking.

"I would like to thank everyone for their help. I felt so ashamed for getting pregnant at such a young age. I thought God was punishing me when I lost my baby, but I understand now that miscarriages happen. Most of all I know God forgives those who are truly sorry for their wrong choices. I can move on with my life now. Today I promise that I will not sleep with another boy." She giggled. "I mean a *man* - until I get married, because by then I will be a woman." She giggled again.

Shayna listened as the child in Juliana showed. She could not believe Michael had manipulated this girl into giving up her innocence. The more she thought about it, the angrier she became at him.

Cherralyn and Maria gave Juliana a hug.

"Enjoy your childhood. When it's gone, you can't get it back," Cherralyn told her.

"Yes, ma'am," Juliana said with a smile.

Maria told Cherralyn to thank Jasmine for telling them about the center.

"I will," she promised.

Later that afternoon there was a knock on Cherralyn's door as she worked in her office.

"Come in," she said.

James entered and took a seat.

"Have you heard from Jasmine?" she asked.

"I talk to her regularly, but she still won't come home or tell me where she is. I've tried to tell her we can't fix our family while she's gone."

"What about Stephen?" Cherralyn asked.

"He's tried to contact her, but she won't answer his calls. I'm assuming they broke up, and that's another reason she's not ready to come home yet. But she looks okay."

"You've seen her?" Cherralyn asked somewhat excited.

James didn't want to go into the details of seeing her on the surveillance video, so he quickly changed the subject. "I saw her briefly, but that's not why I'm here."

"What's on your mind," she asked.

"Shayna."

"What about her?" Cherralyn asked curiously. She could see the concern on his face.

"All the rumors that have been going around about her and Michael," he said.

Cherralyn took a deep breath and leaned back in her chair. "If you already have an opinion formed of her, why are you sitting in front of me?" she asked him.

James did not expect that. He stared at her, and his shoulders slumped.

Cherralyn decided to talk to James like Bracie used to talk to her. She had to make him think about what *he* wanted. "You have been spending a lot of time with Shayna. You still haven't figured out who she really is and what she's like?" she asked.

"Yes, ma'am, I have. She's a kind and beautiful person. She has a loving heart, and..." He stopped talking and smiled.

"If you already know this about her, what is really bothering you, the fact that she was sexually involved with someone else?"

James didn't say anything, but his gaze fell to the floor.

"Are you going to hold that against her or treat her any differently?" Cherralyn asked him.

James sat straight up in his chair and made eye contact with her again. "No, ma'am! I understand she was hurting and didn't have anyone. Michael used her pain to manipulate her to get what he wanted. I... I..." He stopped talking again.

"James, you nor Shayna can undo what has already been done. You have to learn to forgive and move on. She has already done so, in a big way. Whatever it is you don't understand about it, ask her and no one else. Only she can tell you what you want to know."

Cherralyn reached into her drawer and gave James a copy of a poem Bracie had once given her. It was titled, *"Don't Judge Me!"*

James read the poem and smiled.

"Keep it," she said. "I have more."

James stood up and embraced her. "Thank you, Ms. Cherralyn. You always know the right thing to say."

She walked him to the door and then returned to her desk. *"What a day, Lord!"* she said as she looked around her office. *"Please give me wisdom one day at a time."*

Cherralyn finished her work, and then she locked up the center and went home to her husband.

Chapter 13

David and Cherralyn stood in the doorway of the newly decorated nursery.

"We're having a baby," she said and smiled.

David rubbed her tummy. "We did promise Mr. Tyler we would fill this home with beautiful children," he said.

Cherralyn turned and looked at her husband. "I hope you only mean two or three," she said smiling.

"How about five or six?" David said laughing.

"Yeah, only if you-"

He cut her off. "It ain't happening," he said and they both laughed.

David hugged Cherralyn and closed the door to the nursery. They were still laughing and teasing each other as he walked Cherralyn to her car. He bent down to kiss her.

"Tell the kids hello, and have a blessed day. I love you."

Cherralyn kissed her husband and drove off. When she got to the center, she didn't have to wait long before her first visitor arrived. Melanie knocked as she entered Cherralyn's office. Cherralyn saw the concern on Melanie's face as soon as she stepped inside.

"What's wrong?" Cherralyn asked as she walked over to her.

"A Gregory Albright is here to see you, with his lawyer," she answered.

Cherralyn hid her concern so Melanie would not worry. "Show them in," she said as she stood behind her desk.

Two men entered the office. They shook hands with her and introduced themselves. Cherralyn told them to have a seat.

"How may I help you?" she asked as she took her seat. She looked at Greg. "You look familiar."

Greg ignored her statement and slid some papers towards her. "You can start by vacating my house," he said sarcastically with a smile.

Cherralyn looked at Greg and then his lawyer.

Mr. Danbey said, "Mrs. Gray, the Shaws could not give you what was not theirs. Tyler Shaw signed his house over to Mr. Albright before he married Bracie Turner."

"What are you talking about? That is my home!" Cherralyn said to both of them. "I will not give it up to you or anyone for any reason! You will be hearing from my lawyer." She stood up, walked to the door and opened it. "You may leave now."

As the men passed, Greg told her, "You have two
weeks to be out of my house."

Cherralyn closed the door and sat at her desk.
She reached over and picked up the picture of Tyler and
Bracie. "What's going on? They're trying to take the
home that you have given me," she said to the picture.

Melanie entered the office. She could see
Cherralyn was visibly disturbed by the visit. "What's
going on?" she asked.

Cherralyn put the picture back on the bureau.
"They're trying to take my home," she said with tears in
her eyes.

Melanie told Cherralyn to go home and talk to
David. "I'll take care of things here," she said. Melanie
encouraged Cherralyn on her way out of the center. "I'll
be praying for you," she told her.

"Thank you," Cherralyn said.

●●●●●●●

Carl and Shanelle could not believe what they
were hearing. They had come to the house as soon as
Cherralyn called. David told Cherralyn to calm down for
the sake of the baby. They both turned to Carl and
Shanelle.

"What are we going to do?" they asked.

Shanelle was so angry, she was shaking. "The
nerve of him," she said with great hostility.

"We will talk with Kenneth, Tyler's accountant and Attorney Paulding and get back with you," Carl told the couple. He took Shanelle by the hand and they left.

●●●●●●●

Miles away, Greg lay on the bed in his hotel room. *I've waited over 15 years to get that house*, he said to himself. *I deserve it. I worked too hard to let it be taken from me.* He smiled wickedly. *In two weeks I will be living in the type of house that I was meant to live in. I will have the vacation home in Aspen, and all of it is paid for. Life is looking better each day*, he thought.

Greg turned over and looked up at the ceiling. *Tyler never realized he signed over his house or the property in Aspen to me.* He laughed. *Thank God I didn't spend and splurge all these years.* He went to sleep puffed up in pride.

●●●●●●●

Later that week, Greg walked around the production studio with his attorney. *Tyler upgraded very well*, he thought. They were soon shown to the studio's conference room. Greg was not surprised to see Kenneth there. He was at the last meeting between him and Tyler. Greg also expected to see Shanelle and Mr.

Paulding. But he did not expect to see Carl sitting at the head of the table.

"What is he doing here?" Greg asked annoyed.

Mr. Paulding stood and introduced himself to Mr. Danby, Greg's attorney. No one bothered to acknowledge Greg's presence. Kenneth stood between Carl and Mr. Paulding. He placed several folders on the table before asking for the papers Greg had shown Cherralyn a few days earlier. The attorney, Mr. Danbey gave him the papers.

"Everything here is legal and binding," he said.

Greg leaned back in his chair and smiled. He looked at Shanelle and Kenneth and wondered, *What are they so happy about?*

Mr. Paulding gave the papers back and opened one of the folders. "First, this contract is no longer valid," he said.

"And why is that?" asked Mr. Danbey.

"I copied this, so you both can read along," Mr. Paulding replied. "The morning Mr. Albright met with Mr. Shaw, he signed away any rights he may have had. Please go to page two, paragraph three," he said.

Mr. Danbey turned to said page and they began to read: I, Gregory Albright, agree to release ownership of all properties and accounts signed over to me by Tyler Herman Shaw. That includes, but is not limited to, his place of residence at 77029 Dove Court Drive.

Greg read the address, and his mouth dropped. They continued reading: The vacation homes in Aspen, Colorado; Oahu and Kai Lua Kona, Hawaii; Houston, TX; and Venice, Italy. I give up all legal rights and claims to any holdings and stock in T. Wahs Production Studio.

If, at any time, I, Gregory Albright, attempt to attain ownership of any said properties, I give the present holders permission to prosecute me to the fullest extent of the law. The charges include, but are not limited to, embezzlement, fraud, breaking and entering, intent to do bodily harm and/or kill.

Greg could not believe what he was reading. "I did not sign this. I never tried to kill anyone! This is a lie!" he yelled.

Mr. Paulding touched one of the folders, and Kenny opened it. He gave Greg and Mr. Danbey a copy of the papers. They read: I, Tabita Stonewall, do hear by swear under oath that I was solicited by Gregory Albright and paid $5,000 to have sexual relations with Tyler Shaw. I was specifically chosen for the job because Mr. Albright had prior knowledge that I am HIV positive. I was promised to be paid an extra $10,000 if I could get Mr. Shaw to have relations with me unprotected, so he could become infected and therefore infect his wife, Bracie Shaw.

"She's lying! She's a liar and a tramp! Who's going to believe her?" Greg shouted.

Kenneth put a DVD in front of the men. "It was taped when you paid her the $10,000. We have the entire conversation and transaction. Do you need us to play it for your lawyer?" he asked.

Mr. Danbey looked at Greg, waiting for an answer.

"No," he said under his breath. Greg continued to read the papers set before him. "Tyler set me up! He tricked me into signing these papers!" he said angrily.

Kenneth slid another DVD in front of the men.

"What is this?" Greg asked.

Mr. Paulding said without expression, "This is the morning you signed the papers. It shows you reading page one and signing the rest of the legal agreements. It also shows Tyler telling you several times to read the documents carefully before you sign them."

Greg remembered. He was so glad Tyler wasn't prosecuting him, he had hurriedly signed the papers so he could get away from him. Mr. Danbey picked up page one and read it:

I, Tyler Herman Shaw, will forgo prosecuting Gregory Albright on the following charges of forgery and theft. All monies and jewelry obtained by Gregory Albright will be considered gifts. Upon the date that Mr. Albright violates any of the further charges; including, but not limited to, the charges on the following pages and trespassing on any properties owned by Tyler Herman Shaw, Bracie Lynne Turner Shaw or T. Wahs Production, the terms of this agreement to not prosecute will be terminated.

Mr. Danbey turned to Greg and leaned closer to him so the others could not hear what he was saying. "Mr. Albright, you do know that by sitting in this room, you could be giving up your freedom? Mr. and Mrs. Lovett or Attorney Paulding can have you arrested."

Greg ignored his lawyer. "I have not been on any of their property," he said.

"I beg to differ," Shanelle said as Kenneth slid another DVD in front of them.

"You spent your honeymoon at the vacation home in Oahu, Hawaii, and your family has vacationed in Aspen on several occasions. The only reason Tyler didn't have you thrown out and arrested is Bracie asked him not to because of your wife and children."

"Y'all have been spying on me!" he shouted.

Mr. Danbey turned to his client. "Mr. Albright, you seem to have not read anything past the first two paragraphs. Did you ask to have legal counsel present? That can help you now, if they refused."

Before Greg could say anything, Mr. Paulding spoke again. "Mr. Shaw asked if he wanted an attorney present, and he said no. It's on the tape."

"What were you thinking?" Mr. Danbey asked.

Greg touched the scar on his neck and thought back to that Wednesday morning. Kenneth and Mr.

Paulding were standing beside Tyler when he entered the office. Tyler calmly told him to sit down and read the papers on the desk. Once he realized they were not having him arrested or taking back the money he had taken, Greg hurriedly signed all of the papers. He wanted to get out while Tyler was still calm.

By the time he signed the last page and stood to leave, Tyler was standing in front of him. He saw the rage in his face. Greg cowardly fell back into the chair. Tyler reached over and picked Greg up by his throat. Greg's feet were off the floor. He would never forget the anger and hatred in his eyes.

"I trusted you, Greg, and you betrayed me. Because you hurt my wife, you have lost everything." Tyler tightened his hand around Greg's throat. "If you ever come within 20 feet of Bracie again, I will kill you with my bare hands and feed you to the dogs. Do you understand me?" Tyler's voice was full of venom.

Greg only nodded, because he couldn't speak. Tyler threw him to the floor and told him to get out and never come back. He then looked over at Kenneth and called for security. He next called the two crewmen that had cleaned Greg's office.

"Did you remove everything from that office?" he asked.

"Yes, sir," they answered. "We put it all at the front gate, so he could take it with him."

Tyler nodded and they left his office. Security came and escorted Greg off of the premises.

Kenneth and Mr. Paulding saw Greg touch his neck. They thought Tyler was going to kill him that morning.

Greg suddenly became very angry. "Tyler threatened me that day!" he yelled at everyone at the table.

Kenny touched the DVD again. "No, he did not! The confrontation between you and Mr. Shaw did not happen until *after* you signed the papers and you were ready to leave. He never threatened you during the signing of those papers. As a matter of fact, he never threatened you at all," Kenneth said.

Greg knew that was not a threat. He purposely stayed away from Bracie from fear of not only Tyler but her son Anthany.

"Do something!" he yelled at Mr. Danbey. "I paid you to get my house!"

Carl stood up. "Enough! As owner and CEO of T. Wahs Production, I demand that you get off of my property. If you ever set foot in here again, for any reason, I will have you prosecuted to the fullest extent of the law on every charge listed on those papers."

"What?" Greg yelled in shock. "*You*?! Tyler left all of this to his driver?" he said in disgust.

For the first time since the meeting began, Carl smiled. He looked at Greg. "No, not his driver. He left it to his friend. Now get out!"

Shanelle stepped in front of Greg as he headed towards the door. He glared at her. She shook her head.

"Bracie left you something," she said to him.

"What are you talking about?" Greg asked.

Shanelle opened a brown envelope. "Tyler gave the Aspen house to Bracie," she said. "Because she knew your *family* loved the house, she wanted to give it to you as a gift. Tyler was not happy about it, but he told her to do with it as she pleased. They had this drawn up."

None of the men knew about the gift from Bracie, so they stood and listened.

Shanelle read the paper: "I, Bracie Lynne Shaw, being with sound mind, give the vacation home in Aspen, Colorado, located at 14673 Shonto Drive, to Gregory and Anya Albright as a gift. Included in this agreement is the house and the five acres of land the house sits upon. The private account set up to maintain the property and pay the taxes on said property will also be turned over to Mr. and Mrs. Albright.

The only stipulation to this gift is Mr. or Mrs. Albright must ask to purchase it. At such time Shanelle Lovett must release all deeds and claims to said property and account. If at any time Gregory Albright attempts to claim any property owned by myself, Bracie Lynne Shaw, or my husband, Tyler Herman Shaw, by manipulation, extortion or any criminal intent, the terms of this gift will become void.

At such time the property will be released to Living Hope Christian Church for marriage and youth retreats. The use of said property and its account shall be overseen by Shanelle Lovett and Pastor Ryan Jones. This was written, signed and filed in the State of California before the Honorable Judge Charles Henry Turnerbriss. Witnesses are Tyler Shaw, Shanelle Lovett and Vanessa Metonine."

The men looked at each other and then at Shanelle, Greg and Mr. Danbey as they stood in the middle of the room.

Shanelle gave Greg a card. "Read it, and try to live by it from now on," she said.

Greg looked at the card. It read: *Proverbs 16:18 Pride goeth before destruction, and a haughty spirit before a fall. Better it is to be of a humble spirit with the lowly, than to divide the spoil with the proud.*

He looked at everyone in the room. This time Greg knew he had really lost everything. He looked at the portrait of Tyler and Bracie that hung on the wall and left T. Wahs Production Studio with only his freedom intact.

•••••••

Shanelle sat in Cherralyn's office waiting for her to come in. The last time she was in there, she was having lunch with Bracie. She stood in front of the picture with herself, Bracie, Cherralyn, Vanessa and Bracie's daughter Kirnette. Next to the picture hung Bracie's favorite poem, "*I Am A Woman.*"

Shanelle thought about the day they all took the picture at Bracie's home. She smiled as she thought about how they were all present when the picture and poem were mounted on the wall. Bracie told them, "Remember, being created a woman is one of the highest gifts God has bestowed upon us. He has entrusted us with so much. He has given women one of the greatest responsibilities in life; creating, nurturing and raising up Godly families."

Shanelle saw the picture of Tyler and Bracie sitting in the same place Bracie kept it on the bureau. She sat down and stared at it. By the time she decided to reach over to pick it up, Cherralyn entered.

"Sorry, I was just looking at their picture," she said as she put the picture back in its place.

"It's okay," Cherralyn replied as she sat at her desk.

Shanelle smiled. "You don't have to worry about anyone trying to take your home. Mr. Albright will not be bothering you again."

"Thank you so much, Ms. Shanelle. My home is very special to me, and I didn't want to lose it, I was so worried."

"He's been taken care of," Shanelle replied.

"His face looked so familiar."

Shanelle gave a slight laugh. "He used to work for Tyler years ago."

"Oh," was all Cherralyn said.

They both glanced at the picture at the same time.

"I miss them so much," Cherralyn said as tears filled her eyes. "How can I ever thank them for the love and kindness they gave me?"

"Keep running the center with love and compassion, as Bracie did," Shanelle answered.

They were both quiet for a moment.

"I talked with Kirnette," Cherralyn said finally, breaking the silence in the room.

Shanelle looked at her but didn't say anything.

"I wanted to thank her for the scrapbooks." Cherralyn put her hand over her stomach and looked at Shanelle. "I told her David and I would like to name our daughter after her mother, Bracie Lynn." Cherralyn could barely speak through her tears. "I love her so much. She and Mr. Tyler mentored David and me through some rough times in our marriage. She taught me how to love myself and to know that God really did love me beyond my mistakes."

Cherralyn opened her desk drawer and gave Shanelle a card. "This is the card Ms. Bracie sent me the night before she got married. In the midst of all that was going on in her life, she thought about me. I have never forgotten that."

Shanelle let her head drop as she cried.

Cherralyn stood, walked over to her and hugged her tightly. For the first time in a long time, Shanelle let her tears flow freely.

"I miss them too," Shanelle said. "I never told anyone, but when I found Tyler, he had a card placed over his heart. It was one Bracie had given him when they first got married. I kept it and put it in their wedding album that's sitting on my vanity. Tyler was very blessed to have her in his life. She made him so happy."

"We were all blessed from knowing Bracie," Cherralyn said softly.

They sat next to each other and held hands as they shared memories of the love they'd shared with their friends, Tyler and Bracie. When Shanelle stood to leave, Cherralyn embraced her again.

"Ms. Shanelle, thank you and Mr. Carl for stepping in and helping David and me. We needed that."

"Bracie loved you. You had become like a daughter to her," Shanelle told her.

Cherralyn walked her to the door. "You and Mr. Carl are welcome to attend the grief classes. They really do help."

"We'll give it a try. Thank you," she said as she left.

Cherralyn closed the door. She went back to her desk and put her card back in the top drawer. She leaned back in her chair and closed her eyes. She prayed as tears began to fall down her face again.

"Heavenly Father, thank you for blessing me to be a part of Ms. Bracie's life. Thank you for loving me through her. Help me to mentor and touch the life of every person who comes through these doors. May my life be a beacon of light to all who enter looking for help. May I always direct them to you."

She touched her stomach. *"Father, help me to raise our daughter in the fear of Thee, and may she grow to understand and embrace the reason for which her name was chosen. Amen."*

Cherralyn locked up early. She went HOME to celebrate with her husband.

Chapter 14

Jasmine sat in the park. It was quiet, and no children were on the playground. The October air was cool, but she was tired of sitting in her tiny room. She bought a few canvases and paint with some of the money she had left.

She sat the easel up and put a canvas on it. Jasmine had not painted in a long time. She looked at the brush and spread the soft bristles across the palm of her hand. She closed her eyes to tune out everything except the scenery around her. Jasmine started painting. She enjoyed the soothing peace painting gave her.

The sun was going down and she didn't realize she had been painting for so long. She was putting away her supplies when a nicely dressed man walked up to her. She eyed him as he got closer. He looked to be at least six feet tall. He had a nice cut and clean face, except for a nicely trimmed mustache. He wore a nice suit and what looked to be real alligator shoes. With her training Jasmine knew she could disable him long enough to get away if she needed too. *I have to be more careful*, she thought as he stopped in front of her.

"May I take a look?" he asked politely as he pointed to the canvas.

She stepped aside. "Please be careful. They're still wet," she said still watching him closely.

He looked down at the other painting and picked it up. He stepped closer to the easel, and they talked about the depths of her paintings. He knew the different strokes she made to get certain effects on the canvas. Then he shocked her.

"I'd like to buy these. I would be honored to hang them in my art class."

Jasmine definitely needed the money. "Okay," she said.

Before Jasmine could mention a price, he offered her $700 for both canvases. He paid her for the paintings with cash.

"Thank you," she said.

"No, thank you," he told Jasmine with a smile and walked off with a painting in each hand.

Jasmine put the money in her pocket, picked up her supplies and went back to her room. She put her art supplies away and began looking for her phone. She wanted to tell James about her paintings. Jasmine soon noticed her wallet was missing.

"Oh no, I forgot it under the bench!" she said out loud.

She ran back to the park and saw her wallet right where she had left it. As soon as she picked it up, she knew no one had tampered with it. Jasmine put the wallet in her pocket and started walking. After a few steps, she knew someone was following her.

Don't panic, Jasmine. Remember your training, she told herself. When the man reached out to touch her, Jasmine grabbed his arm. She hit him in the face and threw him to the ground landing on top of him. As she raised her hand to hit him again, he cried out.

"Jasmine, wait! It's me, Michael!"

She took her knee off of his chest and waited for him to turn his head, so she could see his face. It was him.

"Don't ever do that again. I could have really hurt you!" she said.

"You mean worse than this?!" he said, wiping his bloody nose. "I think it's broken."

She took a look at it. "No, it's not."

"What are you doing in this part of town? Everyone is looking for you," he told her.

"I know. Please don't tell anyone that you saw me."

"I won't. Remember, no one likes me, so they probably wouldn't believe me anyway," he said.

They went back to the park bench and sat down. Michael's nose finally stopped bleeding.

"Are you okay," he asked. "Where are you living?"

"I'm okay. I have a small room near here," she replied.

"How often do you come to this park?"

"When the weather permits, and I'm feeling up to it," she said.

They sat and talked for a while. Michael got her to laugh a few times, and for some reason that made him feel good. The air was getting cooler.

"I'd better go now. I don't care much for the night air," she said.

Michael told her goodnight and to be careful.

"I will," she said.

Jasmine made sure he was out of sight and not following her when she walked away. She hurriedly locked the door when she got to her room. She was glad she had worn her jacket, because her baby tummy was starting to show.

●●●●●●●

Michael started coming to the park on a regular basis to watch over Jasmine. He always made sure to stay out of sight. One afternoon she took her jacket off to help Kaylin on the swing. Michael couldn't believe his eyes.

"She's pregnant! That's why she won't go back."

He continued watching her as she played with Kaylin. She seemed content, but he knew she had to be scared. One day he watched her as she sat painting.

When she took a break, Michael got closer to see what she was eating. Crackers with cheese. He remembered Jasmine saying she hated cheese crackers. He continued to watch as she drank a small container of milk. He took a deep breath and left the park.

The following day, Michael stood inside the Welcoming Center looking at Tyler and Bracie's portrait.

"May I help you?"

Michael turned to see Shayna standing there. Her attitude changed quickly when they locked eyes.

"What do you want?" she asked rudely.

"Hey, Shayna," he said politely.

"I said what do you want?!"

"I need to speak to James. Please," he said.

"For what, so you can tell him lies about me?" she yelled.

"Lie on you about what? Is he here? If not, I can leave and talk to him later," he said, growing agitated with her.

"How could you? You take people's innocence as a game?" she continued to yell at him.

"I don't know what you're talking about!"

"Yeah, you always try to play innocent. How could you do that to Juliana? She is just a child!" she shouted at him.

"Stay out of what you don't know, Shayna," he told her, getting angry.

"Everyone knows you got her pregnant and then said it wasn't yours. You took advantage of both of us!"

"I never forced you to do anything," he told her. "Don't stand there trying to play the helpless victim. Remember you came looking for me, too."

"You make me sick, Michael!"

He watched her for a moment and then shook his head. "Look, I didn't come here to see you, so please leave me alone. What happened with us is over. Let it go," he said calmly.

"Let it go?! You get what you want, and then you come in here to start trouble, and I'm supposed to just let it go?" she screamed at him.

Michael didn't answer her.

"You are scum! That's what you are, scum!" she said angrily.

Michael stepped up to Shayna and looked down at her. "So what does that make you?" he said with contempt.

Shayna drew back and tried to slap him.

Michael caught her hand. "Don't ever put your hands on me."

"Stop it!" Cherralyn called to the two of them.

Michael threw Shayna's arm down with force, but not enough to hurt her. Cherralyn turned to Shayna.

"Go wait for me in my office!" She was very upset.

Shayna was about to speak.

"Save it! Go now!"

Shayna had never heard Cherralyn raise her voice or show signs of anger. She turned and walked to the office, feeling defeated and ashamed.

Cherralyn turned her attention to Michael. "First, let me apologize. I'm sorry that happened."

"Yes, ma'am," Michael replied.

"I heard you say you came to see someone else."

"I came to see James Harper," he answered.

"He hasn't come in from school. Is there something I can help you with?" she asked.

Michael looked at Cherralyn. He could almost feel the warmth and compassion that showed on her face. "No, ma'am. I'll catch him later." He turned to walk away, but Cherralyn called his name.

"The Outreach Center is here for whoever needs it. You are always welcome to come by and talk," she said with kindness.

"Thank you. I'll remember that."

"By the way, my name is Cherralyn Gray," she said with her hand out.

"Yes, ma'am. I know. Everybody knows who you are," he said with a smile. Michael shook her hand. "Ms. Cherralyn, I don't know how much you heard just now or what you've been told. I didn't go looking for Juliana. She found me and lied about her age."

Cherralyn could see and hear his remorse. "I know, Michael." He stood speechless for a moment, at the fact she believed him.

"Just remember what I said," Cherralyn told him. "You're always welcome here."

Michael nodded and left the building.

Cherralyn watched him leave and then went to her office. She walked behind her desk and looked at Shayna. "That was unacceptable, and it will not be tolerated here!"

"Yes, ma'am. I just couldn't believe he was trying to be so innocent," Shayna said.

"I could say the same about you," Cherralyn told her.

Shayna looked up at her, surprised by her words. Cherralyn knew she would have to teach Shayna the same way Bracie had taught her, with the painful truth. "Michael told you several times he didn't want to see you, but you wouldn't stop. What he needed to see James for was none of your business. Neither was the situation between him and Juliana. You were out of line, and you have to stop putting all the blame on Michael for what happened," Cherralyn said firmly.

"Why should I?" Shayna said and started to cry. "He took my virginity and then called me trash when he didn't want me anymore!"

Cherralyn walked around her desk and leaned against the front of it. "No, he did not take your virginity. For whatever reason, you *gave* it to him. He did not force you. You were a willing participant in that relationship."

Shayna sat crying. "I feel so ashamed," she said with her head down.

Cherralyn sat next to her and lifted her head. "You can't heal until you accept responsibility for your actions. God forgives, and when He does, He removes the shame. You cannot undo what has been done, but you can move on. In order to have a good relationship with James, or anyone else you must forgive your mistakes, learn from them and press forward."

"He called me trash, Ms. Cherralyn." She started crying even harder.

"I was in the restaurant that evening when Michael came in. It was obvious he had been drinking. He said a lot of things he probably doesn't remember. He did not disrespect you today, even though you were very rude to him. The most important thing is to know that you are not trash."

Shayna only nodded.

Cherralyn stood up and leaned back against the desk. She could see Shayna was hurting, but she knew she had to be told about her behavior.

"You were wrong for trying to hit him. No matter how upset you become, never put your hands on anyone else, especially in this center. Do you understand?" Cherralyn spoke sternly. "He would have had every right to defend himself and hit you back."

"Yes, ma'am," Shayna said.

"You may go now," Cherralyn told her.

Shayna gave her a hug and left.

Chapter 15

Jasmine sat on her bed. She was startled by a light knock on the door.

"Who is it?" she asked softly.

"Jasmine, it's me, Michael."

"What do you want?"

"I have something for you. It's okay, I promise," he said.

Jasmine opened the door slowly. By the time Michael stepped, in Jasmine could smell the food.

"What's this?" she asked.

"Well, let me see," he said as he put burgers, fries, shakes and two apple pies on the table. "Dinner for two." He smiled at her.

Jasmine stood there not knowing what to say or do.

"Sit down and eat," he said, taking her by the hand.

Jasmine sat down and said grace. "Thank you."

Michael could tell she was nervous about him being in her room. "Look, my nose is back to normal," he said with a smile, hoping she would relax.

Jasmine smiled back and began to eat her food. Michael watched her eat. He could tell she was very hungry and must not have had a good meal in a while. When they finished eating, they sat quietly for a moment.

"Okay, what do you want from me?" Jasmine asked.

Michael was startled by her question. "Nothing," he answered firmly.

She looked at him suspiciously.

"You are the first girl that has taken time to sit and talk with me," he said honestly.

"You mean in the park?" she asked surprised.

"Yeah. Do you realize we talked for almost two hours?" he asked.

"No, I guess I was enjoying the conversation," she said. "How did you find me here?"

"I saw you painting. One evening your arms were full, so I followed you to be sure you were safe."

"Oh," was all she said.

They sat and talked for a while. When Jasmine started to yawn, Michael realized she was tired, and he had left. Jasmine noticed he left a bag on the table. He bought her a couple of honey buns, a container of orange juice and a sandwich.

Thank you, Michael, she said to herself. When Jasmine finally lay down for sleep, she was full for the first time in a long time. *"Thank you, God. I was so hungry, and you made a way."* She said, *"Amen,"* and went to sleep.

•••••••

James, Stephen and Shayna went into the art studio at the university. Professor Hargrove stood and shook hands with each of them.

"My sister is assigned to be a student of yours this semester. She left home before school started, and I wanted to know if she's been to class."

"What's her name?" he asked.

When James said her name, he looked through his grade book.

"I'm sorry, son. I see here she is enrolled, but she's never come to class."

James said thank you and turned to leave the classroom. He stopped in front of two paintings on the wall. "Where did you get these?" he asked. He was near tears.

Stephen and Shayna walked up and stood in front of the paintings.

"They're beautiful!"

"What's wrong James?" they asked, seeing he was visibly shaken by the paintings.

"That's the signature our mother taught Jasmine," he said.

The paintings were signed *Jazzy*, her nickname. Professor Hargrove told them about the park where he had purchased the paintings from Jasmine.

"Please tell her to hurry to class, talent like hers shouldn't be wasted," he said with a smile, glad he could help them in some way.

Chapter 16

Carl and Shanelle were sitting in grief counseling. This was their third week, and Carl still sat quietly as everyone shared their stories. When the counselor started talking again, Carl's thoughts drifted off.

In his mind, he and Tyler were sitting in the garden watching their wives sit on the side of the pool. Carl watched Tyler as Bracie's laughter caused him to smile her way.

"What's your secret?" he asked.

"Secret to what?" Tyler replied amused.

"The love between you and Bracie. It's evident, without you ever saying a word. How can I get what y'all have with Shanelle?"

Tyler looked at Carl. "Love her from your soul. I don't worry about giving Bracie one hundred percent, because even that is imperfect. I love her with the love of Christ. I honor her for who she is; my soul mate, my lover and my best friend. Stop searching for what's already in you."

"How do I show her how much I love her?" Carl asked.

"That's your problem. You're trying to *show* her. Just live it, and it will show. Embrace her for the vessel that she is. No matter how strong she appears, in marriage, God says she is the weaker vessel. You are the head. Cover her in prayer. Let her know you are her spiritual cover by living it at all times," Tyler told him.

"I don't know how to handle it when we disagree. I want things to be happy all the time," Carl said seriously.

Tyler laughed, but not mockingly. "You ask for what is impossible. Bracie and I disagree, but we also respect each other's opinions. I will give you one of my best kept secrets," Tyler said as he leaned closer to Carl. "I never allow Bracie to feel our disagreements are stronger than my love for her. Whenever the issue is not solved by bedtime, I make sure to make love to her." He watched Carl's eyes. "Passionate love."

Carl nodded with a smile, "I got it now."

"Mr. Lovett..."

Carl didn't realize that the counselor had called his name several times. He looked up at him.

"How have you allowed yourself to grieve since the Shaw's passing?" the counselor asked.

Carl shook his head as tears welled in his eyes. Shanelle sat looking at her husband. She realized she had never seen him cry or heard him say anything about losing Tyler. She reached over and took his hand.

"Tyler was more than my friend. He was my brother," Carl said as tears rolled down his face. "I still find myself calling his phone when I need advice. It has been so hard."

David came over to Carl and touched him on the shoulder.

"It's okay, man. I understand how you feel." David squatted down and leaned in close to him. "It's okay to cry. Your tears will give you strength and help ease your pain." David stood and asked the counselor and Cherralyn to give the couple the privacy they needed.

Shanelle kneeled in front of Carl and took him into her arms. She didn't say a word. She held him and let him cry. The more Carl released his tears, the more she prayed for him. As much as she loved him, she knew that the only One who could ease the pain in his heart was God. So she called on Him with every fiber of her being.

Chapter 17

Michael and Jasmine were sitting in the park talking and watching the children play.

"I don't want to pry, but how far along are you?" he asked.

"Twenty two weeks," she said.

Michael looked at her puzzled.

"Oh, sorry, five and a half months," she said and laughed.

"Stephen?"

"Yeah," she replied. "He doesn't know. No one does." Jasmine was shocked by his next statement.

"As the father, he has the right to know. If it were my child, I'd want to know," he told her.

She didn't say anything after that. They just sat quietly on the bench.

"Hi, Ms. Jasmine," Kaylin said as she waved at them.

Kaylin's mother was a few steps behind her, as usual.

"She's okay, I'm not leaving anytime soon," Jasmine told her mother.

"I'll be right here," her mother said as she sat down with a book.

Jasmine looked at the title of the book. *The Realest Ever? That looks interesting*, Jasmine thought to herself.

"Guess what!" Kaylin said. She stood in front of Jasmine to get her full attention. Before anyone could respond, she jumped in excitement. "I got baptized at church!"

"You did?" Jasmine asked. She was excited for her.

"Yes, I did! That means I know Jesus died for me, and I am saved!"

"Do you know what else that means?"

Before Jasmine could tell her, Kaylin said, "That means God loves me no matter what! If I mess up, I can tell God I'm sorry, and He will still love me no matter what. Mama says I have to mean it in my heart, when I say I'm sorry."

She stood in front of them with a big smile on her face. "Mama, Mama!" she called excitedly.

Kaylin's mom rushed over. "What's wrong?"

"God loves Ms. Jasmine too, huh, Mama, huh?" Kaylin was very excited!

"Yes, Kaylin. God loves Ms. Jasmine, too," her mother said with a smile.

"No matter what!" Kaylin said, getting more excited as she talked. "See, Ms. Jasmine, God loves you too, no matter what. Guess what?"

Jasmine grinned at Kaylin as she got on her tiptoes to hug her. "That makes you my sister, Ms. Jasmine, 'cause God loves you, too." The little girl hugged Jasmine very tightly.

"Thank you, Kaylin. You're right, you are my sister in Christ now."

"*Yay! Yay!*" Kaylin jumped up and down. Then she stopped and stood quietly.

"What's wrong?" her mother asked.

Kaylin stood in front of Michael. "Hello, my name is Kaylin," she said and stuck her hand out to him.

"My name is Michael," he told her as he shook her hand.

Kaylin stood tall. "Mr. Michael, God loves you, too. No matter what!" She smiled.

"Thank you, Kaylin." He was clearly startled, but he managed to smile.

Kaylin continued laughing and jumping. "Yay! Yay! God loves us, no matter what!"

Her mother looked at the both of her new friends. "She is so excited about being baptized. I pray her excitement in knowing God never leaves her. You two have a blessed day."

She took Kaylin by the hand and walked to the playground. Michael and Jasmine sat quietly on the bench once again, but this time they were silent for a totally different reason.

•••••••

Michael went to his friend's house. No one was in the den, so he went in there. He sank down on the sofa, hoping no one would bother him. Terrance followed him to the room. Michael started to leave when he saw him, but Terrance told him to sit down, because they needed to talk. Michael didn't argue. He sat back in the chair. When Terrance closed the door and turned towards Michael, he did not look happy.

Michael sat up. "What's wrong, man?"

"You tell me!" Terrance answered sharply.

Michael looked at him and shook his head. "Say what's on your mind."

"What have you been up to?" Terrance asked.

"I've been looking for a job and spending time with a friend."

Terrance sighed. "Mike, I love you like a brother, but I don't have the money to get you out of trouble again."

"Trouble? I'm not in any trouble. I'm trying my best to stay as far away from trouble as I can," Michael replied.

"Come on, Mike. I can tell something is bothering you."

"What are you talking about?" Michael asked puzzled by the tone of his voice.

"I saw you in the park a few times with a young lady. She looks under age Mike. Is that your baby?" Terrance was afraid of what the answer might be.

"No! It's not mine. I promise. She needs a friend, and I've been watching over her." He paused for a second. "I do care about her, and I'll just leave it at that for now." Michael had a dark look on his face that Terrance had not seen in a long time.

"Are you okay man?" he asked more calmly.

Michael only nodded as he drifted deep in thought. Terrance touched him on the shoulder to get his attention again.

"Brother, you cannot move forward until you let go of the hurt from your past. Remember, God loves you. He's waiting on you to make the first move."

Michael nodded and stood to leave.

"Mike, please be careful," Terrance said. "I know you've been through a lot. It'll get better."

Michael nodded again and walked towards the door. Terrance gave him a pat on the back and let him pass.

Chapter 18

Michael stood inside the church foyer. He could not get Kaylin's words out of his mind. *God loves me, no matter what,* he kept saying to himself. He had felt differently since that day in the park. He opened the door, went inside and sat down on the back pew. He listened as the choir sang. He listened closely to every word Pastor Jones said during his sermon.

When the doors of the church were opened, Michael stood up but couldn't move. James saw him when he first entered the church. He came down from the choir and took Michael by the hand and walked with him to the front of the church. Shayna and Terrance's hearts were full as tears ran down their faces.

Pastor Jones approached Michael and gave him a hug. Michael asked for the microphone. He asked God to forgive him of his sins. He apologized to everyone at church for all the wrong he had done and for all of the pain he had caused. He stood before God and cried for the first time since his mother walked out on him, his brother and his father.

"I feel like a new person," he said.

Pastor Jones patted him on the back. "That's because you are, son. That's because you are!"

●●●●●●●

It had been raining for three days, so Jasmine had to stay inside while she worked on her paintings. Kaylin's words kept ringing in her head. Jasmine looked at the painting of her parents sitting in God's hand, and tears rolled down her face.

She got up and took a poem out of her wallet. Her mother had gotten it from Ms. Bracie during one of the seminars she hosted at their home church in Florida. *No Secrets Before The Father*. Jasmine's mother explained the meaning of the poem to her on several occasions. Once Jasmine fully understood it, her mother told her to keep the poem close to her at all times, and she had.

Jasmine opened the paper slowly and carefully. She had not read it since her parent's death. When she got to the end of the poem, she fell on her knees and cried out to God. From her heart, she poured out her pain.

Jasmine told God how ashamed she felt for being pregnant out of marriage. She told Him she was tired of playing games with her life, she was tired of being alone and tired of being angry that her parents were gone. She knew at that moment of surrender that she wanted forgiveness; forgiveness from God, her family and her church for all that she had done.

Jasmine got off the floor and sat on the bed. She didn't know how long she had been on her knees crying out to God, but now she felt relief. She read the poem again, and fresh tears filled her eyes.

"Father, I do not want to spend Thanksgiving alone. I don't know what to do next or who to talk to. Please God, help me. Amen."

Jasmine lay down and hugged her pillow. Feeling freer than she ever had before, she went to sleep happy.

She woke up at dawn on Wednesday morning. She prayed and read her Bible. When she finished, she picked up her phone.

"Hello, Bracie Shaw Outreach Center. How may I help you?" the receptionist said.

"May I speak to Ms. Cherralyn, please?"

A song played until Cherralyn picked up.

"Hello?"

"Ms. Cherralyn, this is Jasmine."

"Jasmine, baby, where are you? We have been so worried about you!"

"I know. I'm so sorry." Jasmine began to cry.

"Are you okay? Do you need me to come and get you?" Cherralyn asked.

"No, ma'am. I'm okay. Ms. Cherralyn, I don't want to be out here anymore. I don't want to be alone tomorrow," she said through her tears.

"Jasmine, stop crying. You don't have to be alone tomorrow. We still serve Thanksgiving dinner here every year. You are welcome to come."

"Okay."

"Your family will be here to help serve. I just want you to know, so you won't be surprised by them being here," Cherralyn told her.

"Thank you for telling me. But please don't tell them I'm coming, in case I change my mind."

"I won't say anything, but Jasmine it's time to come home baby. I don't know what's going on with you but God has laid it upon my heart that you really need your family right now."

Jasmine could hear the compassion in her voice. "I know Ms. Cherralyn, but I've messed up so bad," she said sadly.

"That's what family is for Jasmine, to help us live past our mistakes," Cherralyn told her.

"Yes, ma'am, you're right."

"I love you, Jasmine, and I'll be praying that you'll come have dinner with us tomorrow."

Jasmine hung up the phone. Feeling a little relief, she rested her head on top of her arms on the table.

There was a knock on the door. She opened it, and Michael walked in with food. They sat down and ate. After they finished eating, they talked for hours. He told Jasmine about going to church and surrendering his life to Christ. He told her how the outreach center was giving him the help he needed to heal the pain caused by his mother's abuse and leaving their family for another man.

Jasmine talked about her parents and their life in Florida for the first time in a very long time. She told him how grief counseling at the outreach center started helping her deal with the pain of her parents' accident and death.

When she told Michael about the note she left for Stephen's cousin Claudia, he just looked at her. Jasmine lowered her head.

"He has a right to know that you're still carrying his child. Don't take that away from him. God has forgiven you and Stephen, and me, too," Michael said. "We have to let the past go and move forward, Jasmine. Don't keep his child away from him, because he was honest and man enough to tell the truth. He was not mentally or financially prepared to get married."

Michael took her by the hand and prayed with her. After he finished praying, he continued to hold her hand. Jasmine noticed tears in his eyes.

"Michael, are you okay?" she asked softly.

"Yes," he replied. "That's the first time I've ever prayed with or for somebody."

Jasmine squeezed his hand to reassure him he did well and she appreciated it. She looked at him and told him she wanted to go to the center tomorrow. She asked if he would go with her.

"Of course I will."

Michael agreed. He gave her a hug and kissed her softly on her forehead before he left.

Chapter 19

Michael walked into the Outreach Center alone. He looked around to see who was there before walking in and speaking to everyone. When he spotted Cherralyn, he walked over, and talked with her for a moment and left. Cherralyn went to the middle of the room and got everyone's attention.

When Michael returned Jasmine was with him. Janice and James were at her side in an instant.

"Thank you God for bringing my baby back safely," Janice cried. She hugged Jasmine and rocked her in her arms.

Shayna walked up and hugged her friend. James hugged his sister very tightly. Cherralyn joined the group hug. No one noticed that Michael had left the room. When he returned this time, he had Stephen in tow. When he saw Jasmine, tears filled his eyes. When Jasmine noticed Stephen standing there, she opened her jacket and put her hand on her stomach.

Everyone looked at her now rounded stomach. Michael gave Stephen a slight push towards Jasmine.

He walked up to her, and she put his hand on her stomach just as the baby began to move.

"This is our baby, Jasmine?" he asked through his tears.

She nodded. "I couldn't do it," she told him when she could finally speak. "I couldn't get rid of our baby."

"Thank you for coming back," he told her softly with his hand still on her stomach. "We can raise our child together Jasmine. We can work out the details later." He smiled at her and wrapped his arms around her tightly.

Janice and James walked over to them and hugged them. Jasmine turned to her aunt and apologized to her for everything she had done. She promised she would get a job after the baby was born so she could pay her for taking care of the cost of the door and for paying the church the money she had taken. She walked over to Pastor Jones and apologized to him, too. He gave her a hug.

"All is forgiven. All is well," he told her.

Jasmine walked back to her aunt and brother. "When I found out I was pregnant, I thought you wouldn't want me back, but I don't want to be alone anymore. Can I come back, please?"

Janice hugged her. "Of course you can!" She had been praying for months, hoping God would bless her to be able to tell her niece that her house was not just a place of shelter because of the loss of her parents. It was HOME.

Pastor Jones took Janice by the hand and told everyone to grab someone else's hand. When they had formed a big circle, he prayed a prayer of thanksgiving for Jasmine's safe return. He asked God to bless Michael for watching over her, and then he blessed the food.

As they sat down to eat, he offered Janice the chair next to him. "Through it all, God is faithful," the pastor whispered to her.

"Yes, He is," she replied with a smile.

After dinner, everyone stayed to help clean up. Michael was standing alone when Shayna walked up to him. He looked at her as she approached him.

"Look, I don't want any trouble," he told her.

"I'm not going to cause any trouble," Shayna said. "Actually I came over to apologize for last time. I was out of line, and I'm sorry."

They both stood silently for a moment. "Apology accepted," he said to her. "I'm sorry for my part in all that. I guess we were both going through our own issues and didn't know how to handle it, so we kinda used each other to dull the pain," he said.

Shayna nodded and stuck her hand out for him to shake. Michael looked at her hand and pushed it softly away. Shayna looked at him and turned to walk away. Michael called her back. When Shayna turned around, he reached and gave her a hug.

"Friends?" he asked.

"Friends," she replied with a smile and then walked to where James was standing, watching them.

Michael was cleaning up later when he heard Terrance call his name. Michael turned to see his father and brother standing next to Terrance. He walked slowly towards them. His dad reached out and grabbed him and hugged him tightly. Michael pulled his brother into the embrace.

"Dad, I am so sorry for all the trouble I have caused. I wish I could change things, but I'm trying to make up for it," he said with tears in his eyes.

Michael's father hugged both of his sons again. "There is no need to try to fix what cannot be changed," he said. "I love you, Michael. I love both of you."

Michael hugged his dad tighter. "I let go of the pain, Dad, and I surrendered my life to Christ. I'm ready to move forward now. Will you help me?"

"Of course I will. I only ask that you come back HOME."

Michael nodded. He knew then that his life would be different now. He walked over to Terrance and gave him a hug and shook his hand.

"Thanks for always having my back and never giving up on me."

"That's what friends are for. Now let's finish cleaning this place, so we can all go home." Terrance slapped Michael on the back and put a broom in his hand.

When the center was put back in order, David and Cherralyn bid everyone goodnight. As each family left the center, she gave them a poem of encouragement that had been written by Bracie and given to her.

Once everyone was gone, she and David stood in front of the picture of Tyler and Bracie.

"Thank you," they said together. They locked up the center and went HOME!

Chapter 20

Carl and Shanelle parked the car and walked into the studio. They held hands as they walked through each room to inspect the Christmas decorations. It was Tyler and Bracie's tradition to have decorators come in the Wednesday before Thanksgiving to decorate and bring in the studio's Christmas trees.

Everyone knew Christmas was the Shaw's favorite time of year, especially Bracie. Tyler wanted the studio decorated when everyone returned to work the Monday after Thanksgiving. It instantly brought an extra feel of cheer and happiness to all of the employees and visitors, too.

Because blue was Tyler's favorite color, one year Bracie decorated the tree in the Welcoming Area with only blue, white, silver and crystal ornaments. Tyler loved the tree so much, it had become a part of his Christmas tradition at the studio. Each year he and Bracie added a silver or crystal angel to the tree.

Carl and Shanelle stood in front of the tree. "I will honor his traditions," he said as he placed a silver angel on it. Shanelle looked at the crystal angel she and Bracie had made. Because it was too painful to hang last year, she kept it until this year. She took the angel from its container and hung it on the tree.

"Tyler's angel," they said at the same time and laughed.

They walked to the offices to make sure each door had something decorative on it. Carl stopped in front of the door that used to have his name on it. Shanelle looked at the empty slot and squeezed his hand. Carl had his name plate removed months ago. His office was the only door without one. He held Shanelle's hand tightly.

"It's been a long hard sixteen months. It's still hard to believe that Tyler is gone. It's even harder to believe he entrusted all of this to me," Carl said, barely loud enough for Shanelle to hear him. He put his hand on the door for a moment and walked away.

Shanelle followed close behind but did not say anything. Carl stopped in front of Tyler's office. Shanelle stood next to him. She reached up and removed Tyler's name plate from the door. She opened the special box she had made for the plate and placed it in there and closed it. When the lid snapped shut, Carl closed his eyes and talked silently to Tyler. Shanelle stuck her hand in his pocket and took out the bronze name plate she had made for him six months earlier. She knew that's where he kept it. She put the new name plate in the slot.

When Carl opened his eyes, his name was there. He looked down at his wife, as she took him by the hand and opened the door. She smiled and told him, "It's time baby."

Carl stepped over the threshold of his new office, his HOME at T. Wahs Production.

Epilogue

Now that Thanksgiving was over, everyone at the center was preparing for the Christmas holiday and the upcoming year. James and Jasmine were helping with the music for the upcoming program. Michael and Terrance were working with Cherralyn on starting a class for young men between the ages of thirteen and eighteen on how to be Godly, respectful and responsible young men. Shayna was given her own class of six year olds, and Melanie was training Natalia to be a receptionist and host for the center.

Cherralyn sat behind her large desk. She was taken away by the warmth and beauty that filled her office. On the bureau next to the picture of Tyler and Bracie sat a picture of her and David. She set the pictures together, so she could always remember the hard work and love that started The Bracie Shaw Outreach Center and all of the hard work and love it would take to keep it going.

Don't Judge Me

Don't judge me
by the clothes that I wear,
my size, my race,nor
the color of my hair.
          Don't judge me
by the way that I talk.
I may limp or sway,
so don't judge me
by the way that I walk.
          Don't judge me
by the things that I do.
We may not agree on the same issues,
so don't judge me if I don't think like you.
          If you must judge me,
judge me on things that are true,
my faith in God and my walk of holiness, too.
          I know God will be my final judge.
Only He can see my heart.
For the heart of the matter,
is really a matter of the heart.

No Secrets Before the Father

We can't tip around the presence of God
For He neither slumbers nor sleeps.
He is forever watching over us,
 His dear little sheep.
We need to lay ourselves before the Father
And let God truly heal,
The hurt and the pain we've been
Too ashamed to reveal.
We must lay aside our garments
And strip before God in prayer.
He doesn't use modern medicine,
Only His blood is applied with care.
We must learn to let go of things lost in time,
And let God perform a healing
In our soul and on our mind.
We truly don't have long,
Living this life is not a game.
We must surrender to the Father
Spiritually naked and not ashamed.

A Word of Encouragement

Things will at times seem to go wrong,
Never doubt the Lord, He won't let it last too long.
Someway, somehow, when you at least expect to find,
God will send someone, to give you peace of mind.
Don't hold your head down, unless you do it to pray.
You must know God is listening and He will make a way.
When you feel let down and at the end of your rope,
Hold on, God is there. He will give you hope.
I bring this word of encouragement
To be a blessing for your heart,
Hold it there, keep it safe, and never let it part.

ABOUT THE AUTHOR

Beulah Hall Neveu began writing poetry at the age of sixteen. It was her love for poetry that inspired her love for reading. She is now enjoying her new love, writing. Beulah is originally from Houston, TX, where she teaches at her church and received her certification in Women's Ministry at the Southwestern Baptist Theological Seminary. Beulah is also the author of *Bracie*, a Christian love story. Learn more about Beulah and her books at *beneveuwords4you.com*.

Made in the USA
Columbia, SC
13 November 2024

46004178R00080